ESCAPE

Part 3

SYDNEY
HOLMES

ESCAPE Part Three
Sydney Holmes

Published by: Crespi House Publishing
ISBN: 978-1-941591-07-9 eBook
ISBN-10:1-941591-13-2
ISBN-13: 978-1-941591-13-0

www.SydneyHolmes.com

Formatting by Author E.M.S.
Cover design by Karen Windsor-Worrel at KWW Design LLC
Edited by Valerie at Loud Lit Chicks

Published in the United States of America.

DEDICATION

To anyone who has fought to create a life they wanted
instead of succumbing to a predetermined destiny.
This book is for you.
Fight hard, your life is waiting for you.

BOOKS BY
SYDNEY HOLMES

ESCAPE SERIES
Escape Part One
Escape Part Two
Escape Part Three
Escaping With Eve

AWAKENING SERIES
Awakening
Awake

Coming in 2017

ESCAPE SERIES
Cody's Story
Rob's Story

ALYSSA MALONE MYSTERIES
Shoot The Moon
Paradise Awaits
Midnight's Breath
Red Skies At Night

CHAPTER ONE

Her head throbbed as she tried opening her eyes; the small amount of light shining under the door was enough to bring her to tears. Hoping to shield them, she endeavored to lift her too heavy arm as far as she could, only to have it come crashing back down to the floor with a loud slap. With the drugs lingering in her system, her limbs were still too laden to lift above her head. She swallowed, hoping to get rid of the cotton residing in her mouth.

Blinking a few times, she tried stretching out along the floor, brushing up against the walls with both her toes and her hands — *Damn it.* She knew exactly where she was: The Box. Having spent untold weeks in this very box, Rowan was all too familiar with the feel of the place, its dimensions, its purpose.

Rolling over and pushing up on her hands and knees, she groped around the small space. She was disheartened to discover only one thin blanket, no mat, no pillow, no bucket, no water. That would explain why her body felt so sore. She hated to think what she would feel like after the drugs wore off completely. Sliding around on the cold floor one more time, she felt her heart sink as she leaned back against the wall: None of the usual comforts — as she liked to call them — were in here with her.

Waiting for the panic to take over, she was surprised when laughter bubbled up instead. Her head hurt with the effort, but laughing felt almost cathartic. Stupid. Negative. Asleep. She couldn't believe she let herself get in this situation. Struggling to get herself back under control, she wiped the tears from her eyes and drew in a shaky breath.

The last thing she remembered was demanding to see her son. She'd known, even while starting to lose control, that something like this would happen, but she didn't care just then. She needed her son. They'd held her in isolation for too many days without allowing her to see him and she'd snapped. It really wasn't until Jolly laughed at her that she launched herself at him, clawing at his eyes. The rat bastard screamed like a pathetic old man, calling in his most protective followers. All she knew was blind rage and rough hands all over her. She fought until she felt the needle stab under her skin. Now this.

She sighed.

The last time she was in The Box, Jolly had kept her for a full month. At first she didn't mind; she'd been recovering from surgery and wondering how she was going to keep up on her crews, but after that first week, she'd been ready to get back to work. Her crew had needed her and she had been anxious to get back to it and do her part of the hard labor required.

With no freedom in sight, she'd started practicing some yoga poses she and Lina had picked up from a recruit. Still recovering from her tubal ligation, she'd worked slowly at first, but with nothing to do but recover and practice, she was able to perfect some of the poses before being let out. She never forgot how much joy her practice gave her—without her serendipitous introduction to the art she might not have fared so well.

Every day Jolly had come to her, wanting to discuss her "rash decision" to get her tubes tied. She never let on that, other than boredom, she was doing just fine. What he really wanted to know was how on earth she pulled off getting the surgery without him knowing. Her second major act of defiance. She would not birth his babies. Ever.

After a month Jolly had let her out, thinking she had learned her lesson about defying him, when really what she had learned was just how crazy and controlling he was. She'd become more determined than ever to get out. Too bad it took her over ten years to do it. Maybe if she had left earlier, he would have forgotten all about her, and she would be back with Shane.

The door opened, cutting off her thoughts and spilling more light into the small space. Her stomach lurched as she squinted at the assaulting light. Renewed pounding in her head killed all the laughter immediately.

"I'm glad to hear you find your situation so amusing." Jolly's deep voice made her skin crawl.

She didn't speak. She tried opening her eyes but couldn't overcome the light beating her eyelids into submission.

"Rowena, Rowena, Rowena. You have a lot to learn, my child," Jolly clucked at her.

She wanted to tell him off, to yell at him to get the hell out of here, to demand to see her son, but none of that was happening. Her throat was too dry to speak, her head throbbed with just the thought of shouting at him, and her eyes leaked. Her body was not cooperating in the least and she felt defeated. With no other option, she turned away from him and groped for the thin blanket to hide under.

"I can see you're not quite ready yet. I'll just leave you with this, then," he told her.

Rowan heard his footsteps back out and the door close. When darkness settled back over her prison, she sat up and felt for what he had left behind. After her eyes readjusted to the slim beam of light making its way under the door, she saw a tray with a water jug and a glass on it. Sliding across the floor, she sat up and gulped the water, drinking the entire glass before registering the aftertaste.

With her heart racing, she leaned back and took several deep breaths. Fighting to stay awake, knowing that the drug would eventually take hold of her body, sweat poured down her face as the poison worked its way into her system. At first she just felt light headed. Her limbs became heavy, filling with lead with each passing moment. Soon she had to remember to breathe. Panic filled her as she wondered if maybe he was going to kill her this time. *God damn it, Jolly. You will not win.* She held on to those words as if they were a life raft, fighting the drug's effects as long as she could, before blackness filled her mind, chasing out every thought.

• • •

Shane glanced sideways at the clock, wiping the sleep out of his eyes. The blue hue of his laptop cast an ominous glow over the dark room. It was well after two in the morning and he knew he needed to sleep, but damned if he knew how. Downing the rest of his beer, he hoped like hell sleep would just knock him over the head and leave him to slumber right there in his office. Every damn time he got into that bed, it was if it was swarming with ants or spiders. No way he could sleep in it.

Attempting his search one more time, he felt the regret sitting like a stone in his stomach. If only. If only he'd been there. If only he hadn't been so pissy about her questions. If only he hadn't been so wrapped up in his work. If only he'd been more vigilant, more protective. He had let her down and she was gone.

He didn't know where she'd run off to, but he knew she'd left him. He'd given her his heart and she bolted. And she was damn good at hiding, that was for sure. He'd been searching for days and nothing. No Rowan, no Justin, no Lina, no Talia. As if the entire family had just vanished into thin air.

His head smacked the table hard, waking him up. *Fuck!* Rising unsteadily from his chair, he stumbled down the hall. Maybe the couch would be a better venue for sleep. The walls felt like they were closing in on him. He desperately needed sleep and hoped the beer would help.

He knew he needed to get his shit together, but that voice was weak and muffled in his current state. What he really needed was Rowan. Without her, nothing else mattered. He'd had her—she was his Rowan—and he had fucked it up.

Finally making it to the couch, he fell back on it, rubbing his head where he had hit it as the smell of stale beer wafted up at him. He must have kicked over some old beer cans along the way. Shit, one more thing he'd have to deal with in the morning.

Just a few hours of good, solid sleep and then he'd be able to focus and clean this shit up. He needed to find her and fix this. He knew, if only he could find her, he could fix it. If only.

CHAPTER TWO

Rowan didn't even stir as the sun rose high above the desert. Hidden in her dark prison, she slept. As the rest of the community awoke, enjoyed their breakfasts, took showers, and joined their crews for their daily work, Rowan slumbered, her mind drugged and heavy. At first, as the poison was at its peak, even the most disturbing dreams didn't rouse her. But as the hours passed, and her lymphatic system worked furiously to clean her blood, her body twitched and jerked, if only just, trying to free her from her nightmares. She knew she was trapped and wanted desperately to be free again.

Rowena loved when Jolly came to visit her. She would dress up in her best princess dress for him and brush out her long dark hair, but she would always wear her tennis shoes, because even princesses needed to be able to climb over the rocks.

"Rowena Queena! Are you ready?" Jolly's deep voice filled her room.

She squealed and jumped into his arms, loving the way he always smelled of fresh air and the earth. He liked her smell too, she could tell by the way he always inhaled deeply when they hugged.

"Let's go, Little Princess! We have a long walk ahead of us today." Jolly put her down and held her hand.

She beamed under his attention; there was nothing better than being in his company. Jolly was super important and she knew she was special because she got to go on long walks, watch movies in his private room, and even eat with him. And, he told her that she was. Whatever he said was God's honest truth.

Skipping next to him, she tried to listen as he told her stories about the stars. She wanted to remember this time. He often talked about the stars on their evening walks, but Rowena didn't always understand what he was telling her. She vowed to listen hard, but she would get lost. Today she tried to focus on his mouth, willing her brain to take it all in, but the flowers grabbed her attention.

"One day, Queena, you will be a great leader," he was saying when she tuned in again.

"Why do you call me that? No one does but you," she asked him, tugging on his hand so she could watch his mouth while he answered her.

"I named you that. You are mine. My little Queen." Jolly winked at her, squeezing her hand.

"Okay," she said, not knowing what else to say. That was the thing with Jolly, she often didn't know what to say.

They started walking again and Jolly went back to his story about Orion's Belt. She tried to focus but she couldn't see his mouth and his words started floating together.

"When I'm eight I get a kitten!" she blurted out.

Jolly stopped and looked at her sternly before a wide smile spread across his face. "Here I am telling you old man stories and what you really want to talk about is kittens. Tell me about your kitten."

He sat right on the dirt, but Rowena didn't want to get her dress dirty so she sat in his lap. "The cat in the barn is going to have kittens soon and Eden said when I'm eight I

7

can have one. But if I don't feed it and train it to poop outside, I'll lose it."

Chuckling, Jolly told her, "Well, that Eden does know how to run a household, doesn't she."

"And I want to share a room like the other girls do. I want to share my kitten with them!"

Reaching out and holding her chin, he turned her head and looked right in her eyes. "Queena. Having your own room means you're special. You get all that space to yourself. You don't want to give that up, do you?"

She sucked in her breath. She wanted to be special, but she was lonely. She wanted to live with her friends and giggle late at night. Or at least she wanted to share a room with her big sister, okay half sister, but still! Mostly though, she knew she could never disappoint Jolly – if he wanted her to have her own room, she would keep it and not ask again.

"No!" she told him. "I want to be special."

Rowan bolted upright, listening hard. Adrenaline dumped into her system, waking her, giving her clarity. The building shook again, as if something large was smacking into the corrugated siding. After the third hit, her nerves calmed when it became clear it wasn't an immediate threat and the cotton in her mouth became the pressing issue. Groping for the water jug, she wondered if there was poison in there, too. Surely Jolly would understand that at some point she would need water – clean water. And a bathroom, right?

Sticking her finger in the now tepid water, she tasted it. No aftertaste. Slowly, she sipped from the jug. Rowan almost wept with joy as she drank. She wasn't dead, yet. The relief swept in, eliminating the effects of the adrenaline, exhaustion taking over. This time as she fell asleep, she didn't fight it. She happily let her mind wander. Her first thoughts were of Shane. What was he doing right at this moment? Sighing heavily, she let her heart miss him. Knowing this was better for him; she was no longer dragging him into her horrible life. Still, tears sprang to her eyes as she yearned for his strong body next to her, to hear his heart beat against her ear, to feel his large hands holding her.

When the tears splashed down her cheeks, she'd had enough. No more thoughts of Shane. No more thoughts of lost love and what might have been. Better to think back to her childhood. Maybe the drugs had the right idea.

She had the softest fur any of them could have ever imagined. All black with a white nose and three white paws, Boots was the best kitten in the world. No, in the universe! Lina, Jewel and Rowena all snuck into Rowena's room to pet her one more time. They were supposed to be training, but this was so much better.

"Oh, she is sooooo amazing!" Lina fawned over Boots.

"Guys, I think we should get back. They said hide in camouflage, not in our rooms." Jewel stood at the door listening for footsteps.

"I know, but I just had to check on her. I mean, I only just got her a few days ago and I didn't want her to be lonely." Rowena rubbed the kitten's ears and kissed her head. "Come on, Jewel. I'll stand guard. You have to feel her!"

Jewel glanced one more time out the door before changing places with Rowena.

"Oh man. She is soft, isn't she?" Jewel said as soon as she touched Boots.

"I can't believe Eden said you could have her. And in the Big House, too! You are so lucky, Ro," Lina told her.

"Lucky? I had to scrub her bathroom for eight weeks! Eight times I had to clean her toilet. Yuck!"

"Yeah, but still," Jewel piped in, "You always get the

better deal around here. Look at your room. I'd die to get this much space!"

"I'd trade you in a second, but – " she stopped herself.

"Well, well, well. What do we have here?" Cheri stood at the open door, gun in hand.

"Um. It's my fault Cheri. I, I, I – " Rowena stepped in front of her friends.

"She needed to get her gun." Lina jumped in. "And we just got here and we were, um – "

"You forgot your gun? For training? What are you, asleep?" Cheri barked at her.

All three girls gasped at her accusation; none of them wanted to have that come back to haunt them. Being asleep was the worst thing a person could be. That was what they were all fighting against, sleepwalking through life. People on the outside, in World 48, were asleep and brain washed, but on the Ranch, people were alive, awake, aware.

Rowena glanced over at her friends. Jewel was frozen in terror while Lina hid Boots. Looking back at Cheri, she saw the woman glaring at Jewel with an evil gleam in her eye. All the older kids went after Jewel. They all seemed to hate her for some reason.

"Cheri, this was my fault. We are not asleep! We were all hiding together, but then I needed to come back here. Leave her alone!"

As if Cheri hadn't heard a word, she walked in, grabbed a handful of Jewel's long, curly hair, and hauled her out of the room.

"Cheri, stop!" Rowena screamed to no avail.

She followed them out the door, glancing back in time to see Lina closing her door, Boots safely inside. The two of them followed Cheri and Jewel, listening to Jewel cry as she was dragged across the grounds back to the Arena.

Cheri threw her down in front of the Deck House. Although no one could see them, everyone knew that Jolly and Storm were up there watching, taking notes, storing away wrongdoings and failures to be pulled out at just the right moment.

"Look what I found in the Big House!" Cheri called up to the Deck House.

Everyone waited, for what, Rowena didn't know. Jewel was on her knees, dirt covering her pants as tears streamed down her face, her hair a mess of tangles and curls. Lina stood off to the side, barely breathing. Rowan watched as her friends waited in terror for what was to come next.

After what felt like an eternity, Storm entered the Arena. With one look, all three girls followed her back up the stairs to the Deck House platform. Rowena tried to comfort Jewel, but the girl threw off her hand. Instead, Rowena fell back to walk behind the group, not wanting to face Storm.

While Jolly hardly ever got his hands dirty with messy matters such as children not behaving, Storm often acted as everyone's strict parent. She yelled at people and called them names so horrible that Rowena didn't even know what they meant. But everyone told her that Storm did it for their own good; without Storm, no one would grow and evolve, or wake up.

"Why were you in the Big House?" Storm's voice simmered just under a boil.

No one spoke. Lina opened her mouth once or twice, but nothing came out. Rowena was about to speak up when Storm's hand lashed out, landing across Jewel's face with a harsh smack.

"I asked you a question. Why were you in the Big House?" Storm stepped back, arms crossed, glaring at Jewel, waiting for an answer.

Jewel's sobbing was the only sound on the platform. Rowena couldn't take it anymore. "It was my fault. I forgot my gun and we went back to get it. We were on our way back to hide for the troops when Cheri found us."

Storm's glacial eyes found Rowena's, pinning her to the spot with her stare. "You need to stop taking the blame for your so called friends' mistakes, Rowena. Jewel and Lina are on kitchen duty for the week. Jewel, if you drag any more people down your chosen path, I will have no choice but to talk about retraining. Do we understand each other?"

"Y-yes ma'am," Jewel spit out.

"Dismissed."

Rowena thought she missed something. What was her punishment? They got kitchen duty, but she wasn't even addressed. That wasn't fair! The three girls turned to leave, Rowena following last.

"Could have been worse," Lina said, shrugging when they got back outside.

"I hate both of you!" Jewel hissed at them before running off.

Rowena watched her retreat, her stomach churning with guilt at what happened.

"Yeah, but you guys got kitchen duty when I told her it was my fault."

Lina rubbed her back, comforting her, "That's okay, Ro. That how she's punishing you. Making you feel special or something."

Rowan rolled over, hitting her head against the cold wall. Nervous shivers raced down her spine as her stomach rolled. Oh please, don't be sick. Waking up enough to take a few deep breaths, she willed herself not to throw up in such a small space.

The gun was cold in her small, sweaty hands. She was nervous, but knew she could get through the maze without incident. Just last week, she went through it in record time. Storm and Jolly had made a big deal about it; announcing that at ten, she got through the maze faster than most of the sorry sleepers they had living there.

Now she had to do it again, but this time everyone was

watching her, waiting for her to fail. She hid behind the hedge waiting to get her breathing under control. Six targets waited just around the corner. They hadn't changed the course; she had three targets, then a corner, then two targets, a quick turn around and one last one. Just like last week. She could do it again.

"Rowena!" Jewel whisper-screamed behind her, making her jump out of her skin.

"Jesus!"

"I need your help."

"What's wrong?" Rowena turned around, concerned.

"I need to get past you. If I don't come in first I have to meet Jolly, alone — If you know what I mean." Jewel tiled her head, raising her eyebrows as if letting me into some private joke.

"What? I'm not letting you get past me. And I don't know what you mean. You have to go on a walk with Jolly? Can't handle talking about the stars, Jewel?" Rowena sneered at her.

Jewel gave her a blank look. "Stars? No. Now that I'm ten, I have to...never mind. Please. I'll do anything for you. I just can't go back there."

It was the first time Jewel had talked to her in months. "I can't let you win. Storm will know. She always knows." Rowena rolled her eyes.

Jewel looked like she was going to puke. Rowena watched her for a few seconds. What was up with her today?

"I'll tell you what, let's go together. That way everyone will see us and Storm won't get mad at me for not trying. Okay?"

Jewel's face lit up. "Yeah! Okay. Thanks. On three."

They both took positions behind the hedge and nodded at each other before Jewel started to count. Before she even got to two, Jewel was out and shooting. Damn it! Rowena pulled her gun and spun her body into the right place. Around the first corner, she saw the first target, three wooden arms sticking out of the circle. One. Two. Three. All shots made their mark. She sprinted as fast as she could to the end of the run. Rounding the corner, completely focused, she didn't see Jewel anywhere. There were two swinging paper targets hanging from poles. Oh no, Jewel must have just come through here. One, two. Both within the circle. One more to go. Without stopping or thinking about how far ahead Jewel was, she spun back around the other way and bolted to the third and final target. One shot. All she needed was one more hit and she was done for the week. Her heart sank as she zeroed in on her target. The small balloons tacked to the pole were all moving sporadically in the wind.

She took a deep breath as she aimed her gun. Eyes narrowed down her sight, her hand wrapped around the grip, one finger lightly touched the trigger. She waited until her heart slowed down a bit and then slowed her breaths. When she was certain, she paused at the bottom of her exhale and squeezed. The small purple balloon vanished as it broke apart. Yes!

With her heart rate back up, she dashed to the end of the maze. Coming out of the hedge she looked for Jewel, ready to see her smirk, her glowing smile at winning the race. But she wasn't there. Rowan spun in place looking for her, only hearing her footsteps approaching after two full circles. Jewel was just coming out of the maze.

Rowan watched utterly shocked as Jewel passed through the gate a full minute after she did. She ran up to her to ask what happened? She'd been ahead of her, Jewel bolted at two, not three!

"Jewel —"

"I hate you. What's happening to me is your fault," she hissed, marching off holding back tears.

"Wait!" Rowena called after her. She needed to turn her gun in; to get her bullets verified, to get her count and place.

Even Jewel knew that coming in second wouldn't count unless she got verified. Coming in second was damn good, Jewel needed to stand in line and get counted. She needed to go after her, to help her.

"Rowena!" Storm barked.

Rowena spun around to find Storm walking toward her. "Um..."

"Don't stutter child, it's not tolerated. Grace in all things. You, of all people, need to practice that. You did well again. Your training is improving. Jolly and I would like to see you on the mat soon. We'll be watching." Storm nodded and walked away.

Still a little stunned from Jewel's outburst but elated by Storm's praise, she stood in line to get counted. After all of her bullets were counted, her gun turned in, she would try again with Jewel.

$$\bullet \;\; \bullet \;\; \bullet$$

"There's no fucking way, man. I'm telling you, for the last time, she didn't just take off. Something happened." Cody stood over Shane, barely containing his anger.

"Look, Shane. She came down here looking for you and asked for our numbers. That doesn't sound like a woman about to run. That sounds like a person trying to get back to her normal. Did you call her phone?" Rob piped in, keeping his voice calm.

"Yes, dickhead, I called her phone. Only a dozen times or so. It just rings and rings. She didn't even set up voicemail. And now it's dead."

"Let's go check her apartment again. The more I think about it, the more off this whole thing sounds. Get up, asshole. Let's do this." Rob nudged his friend.

Shane had finally started sleeping, but apparently

now slept too much for his friend's comfort. *Jesus, fuck. Could he do nothing right these days?* He got up and followed his buddies upstairs. Opening the door to her apartment, Shane held his breath. For one quick, irrational moment, he thought that maybe he had been wrong all this time and all of her stuff would be in there, along with Rowan.

Swallowing his own insanity, he stepped into the empty apartment.

"The manager said nothing was left but some toiletries. They haven't even done the official clean out yet because she paid till the end of the month." Cody walked in and started opening cupboards.

Rob joined him, searching the floor and cabinets. Shane nodded his head and headed to the back. Starting with her bedroom, he searched the floor and closet. Other than a few receipts and some trash, there was nothing in the bedroom.

He met Cody near the bathroom. They moved into the small space together. Shane checked the shower while Cody started searching the drawers and under the sink.

"Well, look at this, doesn't look like she packed this at all," Cody said as he opened the drawer.

Having searched the small shower, Shane stood over him wondering what treasures she might have left behind.

"Holy shit!" Cody came up with her cell phone in his hand.

Shane's heart sank, "Yeah, but that's what caused the whole fucking problem. She didn't like having a cell phone. Not surprised she left it here."

"Listen. She came down and asked us for our numbers. Whatever she was tripping about before, she had gotten over. She told us she would take it everywhere. She was looking for you. Her running doesn't add up."

"So, if she didn't run..." Shane asked, not wanting to comprehend what Cody had been trying to tell him this whole time.

"Something happened to her, Shane. I don't know if it was Justin, or her sister, or Jewel, but something other than being pissed at your sorry ass made her clear out of here."

"What'd you guys find?" Rob poked his head in the bathroom.

Cody handed over the phone. Rob took it and started messing with it.

"It was only a little over an hour from when we saw her and when you showed up here. That is not a lot of time to clear out her apartment. Even for her. She had help. Hell, we were outside for a while right after she came over. We didn't see her moving shit."

Shane's knees felt weak. All this time he was wallowing in self pity because she had left him. All this time, he had been wrong. She hadn't left him; she was taken.

Chapter Three

Footsteps jolted her out of her slumber. For the first time, Rowan didn't feel foggy. She had a clear head and needed to go to the bathroom. Having no idea how long she had been locked away, she wondered just how long it had been since she had had food or water. Without warning, the overhead light flipped on, blinding her temporarily.

The door swung open as Rowan blinked back the shock of so much light.

"Oh, look at that, you're awake," Jolly practically shouted.

"I need to pee," she stated flatly.

"Tsk, tsk. Manners, my child. Manners."

Attempting to stand she slid up the wall, testing her legs. Smiling through her grinding teeth, she tried again, "Jolly, I would really love a trip to the bathroom. You neglected to leave me a bucket this time."

Jolly stared at her for a moment, his face frozen somewhere between amused and confused. Rowan would take that over rage any day of the week. Pushing off the wall, she walked a few steps toward him.

"I can either pee here, on your feet, or you can take

me to the bathroom," she spoke, her voice saccharine.

"Yes, yes. Let's go then," he offered her his hand.

Walking felt foreign. Her limbs, out of practice, were uncoordinated, but damned if she would take his hand. Once again, she was in this state because of him. How she ever thought he could do no wrong was beyond her. Her first twelve years were lies. Every. Single. One.

Shaking off her instability, she walked, without help, down the long hall to the bathroom. The air smelled stale, untouched, compounding her sense of loneliness. Jolly unlocked the door and followed her inside.

"You're gonna watch me pee?" Rowan asked, incredulous.

The sting against her cheek was sudden and harsh, stealing her breath.

"Is this what World 48 has done to you? Are you now so unconscious and asleep that you would lose all your grace? I should have left you to lie in your own filth."

Rowan's hand rubbed her cheek without thought and she realized he was right. She was caught unaware, completely asleep to her own situation. She never saw it coming. She should have expected it. Should have been ready.

"I'm sorry, sir."

He waited while she took care of business and quietly walked back to her cell. Never did she ask about getting out, about how long he planned on keeping her locked up. She needed to get her head on straight, she needed to remember where she was. She was home, damn it, and it was time she started acting like it.

Walking into The Box, she turned and waited.

Without a word, Jolly shut the door and locked it. Rowan heard his footsteps fall away while the overhead light blared harshly. Slowly, she folded up the ragged blanket and sat on it. It wasn't much of a meditation cushion, but it would have to do.

Crossing her legs and breathing slowly, she settled in. Taking stock of her body first, she was delighted to discover that she didn't feel any lingering effects of the drugs. Her stomach was empty, her mouth was dry, but her bladder was comfortable and her head was clear.

The sting on her cheek brought back so many memories. So many times she left Jolly with this exact sting. Some worse than others. Nothing as shocking as the first time. The first time she saw the man for the monster that he was.

Leaning back against the wall, she relaxed her meditative position and let her mind wonder.

"Rowena. Come in, come in." Jovial as always, Jolly was almost bouncing in his seat as she approached his couch.

His private quarters were always so much nicer than any of the others. His room was large with lots of windows and furniture.

"How's the Birthday Queen? Twelve years old today. How does it feel?"

"I feel all grown up. That's what Eden said. That now that I am twelve, I am a grown up." Rowena's chest grew with pride.

Jewel had been a grown up for months and she was finally back on even ground with her. She knew she was a woman, that had happened a while ago, but now that she was 'of age' the community would treat her like a real adult.

"I'm so glad you feel that way, because I have some big news for you. You are, indeed, grown and ready. I've been waiting a long time to tell you this, are you ready?"

Jolly moved closer to her, his hand sliding along her shoulders, moving the hair resting on her neck. Rowena swallowed hard, not knowing what to say. Her stomach fluttered a little with nervous energy. She nodded her head, waiting for Jolly to continue.

"Queena, I have waited so long for you. I've been watching you and you are ready. We, my child, are to be married," he announced with a wide grin.

She froze, not understanding what he had just told her. Married? Wait, she didn't want to be married, she wanted to be a grown up – to stay up late and to choose what crews she wanted to work on, to eat dinner with the rest of the community.

"Um, what?" she asked him, hoping she had heard incorrectly.

His large hands grabbed her upper arms and he turned her to look at him.

"Rowena, it's time that you become my queen. I've been waiting. We are to be married and you will carry on our legacy."

Rowena watched as his eyes grew large and scary. As if he wasn't speaking to her but through her, he held her tightly and cast his eyes somewhere just beyond her reach.

"Um, no Jolly. I don't want to be married. I want to – " The force of his grip cut her off.

"You do want this, Rowena. You are untainted and perfect. I have been watching over you your entire life. This is your destiny. We are to be married. You will give me babies, beautiful, untainted babies." His voice was rough and dark.

Goosebumps covered her skin as she shivered. Fear gripped her throat harder than his hands, making it incredibly hard to breathe.

"O-Oh-kay," she stuttered.

Rowan bolted awake, no longer enjoying her

walk down memory lane. Yet she couldn't help her sly smile. Even with all of his scare tactics, she never married him. Never gave birth to his babies and never would. She had Justin, her way, her child — not his.

Where was Justin? What were they doing to him? Did they drug him and lock him in a box too? She shuddered at the thought. She only hoped that they would go easy on him, as they really only wanted him to get to her. But Jewel, she would punish him, wouldn't she? No! She wouldn't let her mind go there. She knew Justin could take care of himself. Wherever he was, he was fine. Probably just worried sick about her. She needed to find him, to reassure him that she was fine.

Laying her head back on the folded blanket, her arm shielding her eyes from the obnoxious light, her thoughts went back to Shane. She was ashamed of herself. The Rowan he knew would have never allowed herself to be locked in a closet. She knew she was losing herself here, but couldn't quite grasp how to stop it. Shane would never want her like this. It was for the best, she repeated, heavy with the thought. Shane most likely thought she ran from him. That was good. It was better this way. Shane wouldn't want her like this. No one would.

She used to have some fight in her. Maybe it was filtered out along with the drugs they gave her. Feeling so weak, she squeezed her eyes shut and tried to remember what it felt like to want to fight. To risk it all to get away. As her stomach growled, she wondered how long it had been since she had had any food.

Wondering what on earth Jolly wanted to discuss with her in his private quarters at ten o' clock in the morning, Rowena walked briskly up the path to the Big House. Trying to put on a brave face, she squared her shoulders and kept her feet moving. Glancing around, she took in the air. Winter was definitely the best time of year in Arizona. The air was clean and cool, the bright sun warmed the ground, and the desert felt inviting, not oppressive.

Stopping just outside the house, she willed her hand to stop shaking as she opened the door. Memories of all the other times she had been summoned raced through her head. She wished she knew what he wanted so she could be more prepared.

"Jolly? It's Rowena. Did you want to see me?"

"Queena! Come in, come in."

Queena? Is he back to that? Her stomach squirmed as she stepped all the way into the room. Closing the door with a loud click, her hair stood on end and her insides flipped. Something was in the air, but for the life of her she couldn't recall anything she had done wrong. Taking a few tentative steps closer to his voice, she waited.

"Come here, my child. I'm not going to bite," he told her, sounding exasperated at her caution.

Forcing a smile, she sat next to him on his couch. Jolly pulled her closer to him, holding her hand.

"My beautiful, beautiful Queena, only eighteen years old, yet you've accomplished so much. I'm so glad you came. We have much to discuss."

He smiled and his blue eyes twinkled at her. His wavy, light brown hair fell just past his ears as he raked his thin fingers through it. He looked so charming sitting there on the couch, so harmless. Rowena could tell he was handsome for his age.

"So, first tell me, how are things in the Nursery?"

Smiling, she didn't hesitate to answer him, "The Nursery is great. The kids get along really well and Lina and I have been working hard to get ready for the opening of the Instructary. The older kids are going to love it! They'll be able to read stories and learn math and read about history. All kinds of things."

"Good, good. You have proven yourself to be a great leader — just like I always knew you would be. That's what I wanted to talk to you about."

Her ears perked up, "Okay."

"Given your role in making these fundamental changes with the Nursery and the Instructary, I think it's time we let the rest of these people in on our secret."

Confused, she sat waiting for him to explain what secret he was talking about.

He chuckled, "Come now, Queena, you have no reaction at all?"

"I'm sorry Jolly, but I don't know what you're talking about. What secret?"

Looking aghast, he clucked at her, "The meaning of your name, Queena. It's time these people knew their queen."

Her mouth fell open. Was he serious?

"Um, I. I don't know what to say. Are you talking about our old game?" she tried, hoping he wouldn't catch the lie.

Jolly looked at her hard, then a smile crept across his face that made her hair stand on end; he was not happy, he was angry. Beyond angry.

"I. Don't. Play. Games. Child."

She sucked in a breath. They had gone over this before, but she had hoped he had forgotten about it.

"Why don't you tell me about it. I've just been so busy these days. Jeremy is a wild little boy and I just, just — "

Standing, he started pacing the room. "You are my queen. Your destiny is to help these people, by my side. They need you. I need you. We need to marry and take this flock to the next level."

Panic filled her veins with each word he spoke. Not again. Never again. She watched in horror as he got more and more animated with every word, talking about their marriage and what it would mean to the people. What their children would accomplish, what her life would be like by his side.

Desperate, she thought of all the reasons it would never work. The first and foremost being the idea repulsed her. She would never marry Jolly and have his babies. No, it wasn't going to happen.

"Answer me, child." Jolly was in her face, demanding an answer to a question she hadn't heard. His face contorted with impatience.

"No. I can't marry you. I'm not a queen. That was just a game we played when I was too little to know better." She pushed him away quickly and got up.

Wanting nothing more than to get out and go back to her sanctuary, to her son, she bolted for the door, but Jolly yanked her back by her hair.

"No one says no to me," he hissed in her ear.

The pain was so sharp she could barely breathe as she tried to focus her mind, to answer him the right way.

"I. I. I," she stuttered, hoping he would loosen his grip on her hair.

Jolly's fist tightened, pulling harder. She could hear her hair snapping. "I can't hear you."

"Yes. Yes, I'll be your queen. I just – "

He threw her on the ground before she could finish. What had she done? Did she just agree to marry him? Oh God, what did she agree to? She wasn't even twenty, and yes, she helped build their school, but no one would follow her at such a young age. Surely he would see that.

"I'm just too young!" she blurted out from the floor, "Jolly, no one looks at me and sees a queen. No one will follow me and besides, if we marry they'll all just think I'm a leader because we're having sex. No one will respect that."

The sting across her check was more shocking than a bucket of ice water dumped on her head. The sound was something that she would carry around with her the rest of her life. Her hand flew to the assaulted cheek and she burned with humiliation.

"Watch your mouth. Where's your grace? Your manners?" he sneered at her.

She stood before him, her head held high but her eyes scanning the room for escape routes. The door was too far away, but there were three windows. Two were viable options if it came to that. Taking a few calming breaths, she tried again.

"My point, Jolly, is that I am too young. These people here are not ready to accept me yet. They're still operating with their lower brains, still asleep. I need to be older, more established in the community before they will let me lead them to the light. The flock is not ready."

As much as she wanted to cry, or even grit her teeth, she knew he would hit her again. She had seen it enough times to know. She spoke smoothly and let her cheek sting, reminding her that she was alive.

He watched her for a full minute before speaking. The entire time she remained still, hoping she was holding her body gracefully enough for him. He started to pace again and she followed his movements with her eyes, waiting for his decision.

"I think you are too young still. This flock is not ready and you have too much work left to do. You need tutoring. You are hardening. You need to be a Queen, you need grace and civility. You have neither." He nodded his dismissal.

Not wanting to spend another second in his presence, she ran for the door. As she tried to open it he leapt at her again, spinning her around, his fingers closing around her throat.

"Don't forget, Rowena. You are my queen and I will marry you. You will have my babies. Everything I said will happen, just the way I said it would." He squeezed tighter with each sentence. She couldn't answer him, but nodded her head as best she could. Her eyes felt as if they were going to *pop right out of her head. She held on as long as she could but she couldn't fight forever. Soon everything went black.*

• • •

Fear and adrenaline. That's what constantly coursed through his blood and gripped his stomach. Shane paced his apartment waiting for Cody to get off the phone, again. That was all too common these days: Cody or Rob made calls, traded in favors for information and tracked down leads while Shane paced.

"He fucking lied to us. He doesn't live anywhere near where he said he did. I think I have to sleep with a few school officials now, and the bastard was never anywhere near where we're looking."

Rob coughed, sputtering a bit of water, "Way to take one for the team, bro."

"What do we know?" Shane asked, barely slowing down his pace.

"We know that both Justin and Rowan shared the same trust issues. We need to widen the search area and start focusing on the sister. Talia is not that common of a name, she has a couple of kids, so she's in the system. Somewhere, somehow — we just need to find it," Cody spoke, his frustration level rising.

None of them liked to be outsmarted, and none of them were taking it well. Without any of them even realizing it, Justin had given them just enough information to sound normal, but nothing real, nothing that could lead them back to him.

"Did he really lie, or did he just cover the truth? Think back to the things he said to us."

"Yeah, yeah. I'm working through it."

"You guys do that, and focus on the sister. I think

that's your better bet. Tracking high school records is cumbersome. I'm going to keep looking for this illustrious Jolly," Shane told them while heading back to his computer.

Frustration coiled tight in his lower gut. She was somewhere. What was that bastard doing to her? Sitting down at his computer, he keyed in the website he was reading late last night. The cult awareness network, at a first glance, seemed like a good resource, but he soon learned that a cult owned it. How did that jive? The page seemed to spend most of its content debunking experts such as Dr. Margaret Singer, simply arguing that cults are just a silly label applied to legitimate groups.

After a few more hours of searching, he found a small mention about a Ranch in Arizona run by a group of Gurdjieff enthusiasts. Shane had no idea if that was Jolly's ranch or not. Rowan had never mentioned Gurdjieff by name. Upon further reading, it appeared as if Gurdjieffian followers believed that the key to a better life was to break out of their sleep walking state and transcend to a higher consciousness. The only way to achieve this is by living in a work group. Often they used the term 'work', meaning working on one's self.

Was this Jolly's group? Rowan never mentioned Gurdjieff or even sleep walking. How can there be no information about an entire ranch where horrific things happen to children? How could he have neglected to ask for Jolly's last name? How can any of this be happening?

Wanting nothing more than to scream and throw his computer through a window, he backed up and held his breath instead. Rob and Cody were still in the front and would likely lose their shit if Shane gave in to that need and tossed it. Only when he felt an immense burning in his chest did he allow himself to breathe.

One thing was for sure: he would not give up. He would find Rowan and bring her back. He would not let Jolly destroy all of their lives. This was not how it was supposed to be, and damned if he wasn't going to fix it, or die trying.

CHAPTER FOUR

Sipping her cold tea, Rowan studied the left corner of her room. Yesterday she counted the holes in the ceiling and discovered a manufacturing defect in three of the panels. All of the panels had 455 holes in each square, except three that had 450 holes. At first she couldn't see a pattern, but after four hours she saw it and realized that the lack of consistency could only be from a mistake when the panels were made.

Today, as she studied the left corner, she hoped to find yet another intriguing mystery to solve. Funny things happen to a person when their entire world becomes less than 350 square feet. After the initial shock, everything slows down. Eight weeks ago the thought of counting holes in a ceiling for hours on end would have made her want to go mad, but now it seemed a good use of her time.

Better than waiting for Jolly to bring her Justin, as he'd promised when she first arrived. Better than living in a box. Better than mourning her life on the outside. Her memories were fading, too. Maybe it was the drugs, but she had stopped dreaming of Shane a few weeks ago and now only thought about him a few times a day. Thoughts of Justin clouded her mind, but she knew letting the worry distract her would only bring more fury from Jolly.

Slowly, she had been clearing her mind, uncluttering her thoughts and checking her emotions. Now, meditating for hours was pleasing to her body and euphoric for her mind. When she felt the need to move, she practiced her walking meditation and yoga. At first she felt her muscles resisting the change, craving more exercise, now, though, she couldn't imagine how active she used to be.

When her time in The Box was over, she had been moved to a new room, one she had never seen before. Truth be told, she wasn't even sure what building she was in. Nothing seemed familiar. They took her out late on a moonless night; she was so weak she could barely walk. When they arrived, nothing looked the same to her. This new room was far from the Big House, but close to Jolly's inner circle.

Jolly seemed to have changed too. He was harder now, colder, more controlling than ever. He was always controlling, but used to have a way about him that made you feel like you wanted to do his bidding. That façade was clearly gone.

Rowan was so tired. For weeks she and Jolly had been having the same conversation. She would ask for her son and he would tell her she wasn't ready to see him. She would ask what she needed to do to get ready, and he would tell her when she knew that answer, she would be ready. She had already spent hours trying to work out what he wanted from her, but lately found it much more appealing to spend her time solving the mysteries of her surroundings.

"And how are we doing this afternoon?" Cheri's voice interrupted her thoughts.

Rowan cleared her throat before answering. She

hardly spoke these days and found that her voice box needed a little warm up before it worked quite right. "Is it the afternoon already?"

"You're so funny, Rowena." Cheri laughed as if Rowan had just made a joke. "I've come to clear your lunch dishes and clean for you. Jolly is planning to visit later and you know how he likes his environment clean."

Rowan watched her as she started cleaning the room. This was a privilege, she had learned, to clean her room. Rowan wasn't allowed to clean or dust or even make her own bed. She was instructed to do nothing. To sit and contemplate her place in this world and all the ways she had led herself astray.

What she hadn't figured out was whether the women who came in to clean were aware that she was here against her will or if they thought she wanted to be kept hidden here. That was what she had been dying to know a few weeks back, but now she figured it didn't matter anyway. She was here. This was her place in life. In this room. Not out there. Not with Shane. Not with the only person she had ever loved. No, it was right here.

If only she could find Justin. That was her only anchor, the one thing that kept her from drifting off into a bliss of constant mediation where her mind remained blank and her body compliant.

Rowan sat on her meditation pillow and closed her eyes. She listened to the sounds of Cheri cleaning, sheets stripped off the bed, covers thrown back over new ones, dust picked up and dirt swept from the floor. Without a word, Cheri made her way to the private bathroom, humming quietly as she closed the door. Still, the smell of cleaning chemicals drifted into the room.

The strong scent reminded her of her old job. How many times had she cleaned the bathrooms at Fresh Greens? Her mind jumped to one of her first days, when Shane came and sat in the lobby waiting for her. Shane. Her brain felt electrified all at once. Her muscles clenched as thoughts of Shane ran rampant in her mind.

Slowly, they faded, and when Rowan opened her eyes, she was surprised to find them wet with tears. Exhaustion took her by storm. She crawled back to her bed and collapsed on top of it. She was asleep before Cheri even came back out of the bathroom.

• • •

"About fucking time!" Cody walked into the office holding his phone.

"What's up?" Shane asked, not looking away from his computer.

"That was Justin. He's on his way here. He finally got word that Rowan is missing." Cody sat heavily in the chair.

"No shit?" Shane looked up.

"We found his aunt. The little shit—I'm still pissed he made us waste a ton of time looking in the wrong place. Anyway, we found him and he's on his way now."

"Good. I can't get an address on this cult. Well, I get too many addresses, so I need to narrow it down. This is killing me. When's he gonna be here?"

"Soon. Like in a few hours."

Shane nodded and went back to his computer screen. He had only taken a few cases since he realized Rowan had been taken. At first he didn't think he was up to it, but his partners needed him so he joined them when they asked. It felt good to get back in the saddle. But now, with Justin on his way, his current cases needed to be done and filed as soon as possible. Shane was determined to find out what had happened to her and wanted nothing to get in his way.

Justin was coming back, he was narrowing down possible addresses and locations, and he knew a fuck of a lot about how cults operate and recruit. Cults, or intensive groups as they are sometimes called, are terrifying. These people don't think like the rest of society. Their loyalties and sense of survival are completely different than anything he'd encountered before.

What he didn't know was specifics about Jolly and his people. What were his ticks, what did his following believe, what were they recruiting for? It seemed that every group had a thing. A lot of them were really about sex. Sex for the leader, that is. But the followers were there for a reason. Some of them were there for a higher purpose, religion, saving the world, attaining enlightenment. Some groups were all about the way of life, plural marriage, power, being just a little bit different, and a little bit better than the rest of us.

What he needed to know from Justin was what makes this group of people special? What was their secret to living a better life that no one else knew? Every group had one; he needed to find out what made this group work.

~

"Dude! Long time no see. You ever thought of calling?" Cody greeted Justin at the door.

"Sorry, man. I just figured everything was fine." Justin looked beat to shit. His eyes were blood shot and he looked exhausted. He seemed tense, angry, and a little ashamed.

"Let it be. He did what we told him to. We told him to go and leave Rowan in my care. He did exactly that. Leave him alone." Shane stepped in the hall defending him, waiting for Justin to give it all back to him for letting those fuckers take his mom.

"I know, I know. I'm just giving him a little shit." Cody backed off and sat on the couch.

"Justin. What do you know?" Shane asked him when he got settled.

"We got word that they had Rowan and I called Cody. What I heard is that they told her they had me and she went willingly." Justin hung his head and took a deep breath.

"Who's talking to you?" Shane asked.

"We have a few friends that sneak out and talk to us. Cheri and Talia used to be best friends before she left. Now they get to talk about once or twice a year. Cheri sent a postcard to the house. That's all I know." Justin spoke with his head down, rubbing the back of his neck.

"Okay. So you trust the source?" Shane asked, a little harder than he meant to.

Justin looked up. "Yeah. Cheri's cool. She's never been too serious about the whole thing, just really likes living in the community. She's not a Jolly fanatic like some of them."

"How serious are those types?" Cody asked him.

"There are definitely some people that would do anything for Jolly. But there are some who would do anything for Storm, too. She has her own inner circle. They play off each other—Storm and Jolly. Between the two they keep the group pretty unstable."

"Jesus," Rob muttered.

"Jolly's really the one you need to watch out for. He's the one who started all the self-defense, weapons training. Storm is much more into intellectual pursuits. Rowan tried to bond with her when she was in charge of the school, but Storm never wanted anything to do with her. It was like Jolly put a claim on her or something."

"So Storm is a leader too?" Shane asked him.

"Yeah, kind of. I don't really know. I left when I was a kid. But I know that a lot of people were more afraid of her than Jolly. Everyone loved Jolly. But Storm made all the rules and would even call out Jolly if he did something wrong. Mostly someone else took the blame for whatever the transgression was, but still, it seemed like Storm was really in charge."

"So Storm knows about this obsession Jolly has with Rowan?" Rob asked.

"Ya know, Jolly always had a lot of women around him. It seemed like Storm left that alone. Even when Jolly was ordering young kids to marry and 'tutoring' the girls on marriage. I heard things from some of my friends. Storm never called him out on any of that stuff. Just like leaving a mess in the kitchen, talking to the wrong people, answering the house phone. Stuff like that." Justin sat on the couch and leaned back with his eyes closed.

"Okay, so why hasn't anyone ever reported this shit?" Shane was beside himself.

Justin laughed, "Shane, you really don't get it, do you? There is no outside. Growing up, there was the Ranch and then a void. We are all taught to loath World 48 — that's this place. There are no resources on the outside. Did you do any reading on mind control? It's not a joke. It took me a solid year to break from it, a year after I left. People may whisper about it, but there is no Child Protective Services or police or anything. Once you're in, you're in — they take your entire mind. Are you getting this?"

"Yeah, I'm starting to. Jesus."

"Reporting to the outside would never occur to anyone. It's just not going to happen, ever." Justin ran his hands through his thick spiky hair.

The room fell silent. Shane knew what he had to do. He couldn't dwell on what might be happening to her, he needed to act. Now he just needed to pry the information out of Justin and get his business in order. He wanted something to come back to when he was done. He hoped he wouldn't return alone.

Chapter Five

"I see you've been sleeping again." Jolly's voice filled the room, waking her with a jolt. Rowan sat up and came face to face with the man sitting on her bed.

"I was taking a nap. After sitting in this room for so long, I don't have the strength to stay awake for more than a few hours anymore," Rowan hissed at him.

Jolly smiled, but his eyes were cold. "Sleeping is good for the mind. It helps correct its wandering ways. Sleeping is," he paused as if he was gathering his thoughts, "Good for the mind, body, and soul."

"So is exercise and fresh air," Rowan growled at him.

"So is respect. And that is something I'm not seeing from you," he chastised her.

Rowan took a deep breath and reined in her anger. She knew that arguing with Jolly was futile. "Sorry. You startled me."

He didn't speak for a minute, making Rowan wonder if that was the right thing to say. She tried to clear her head but couldn't get past the exhaustion. Forcing herself to move, she got up and started walking around the room.

"Where's Justin?" she asked, turning around and looking at him from across the room.

Jolly looked tired. His dark, usually wavy hair fell straight today, as if the hair itself was too tired to curl. His once jovial face was drawn and furrowed, and his shoulders were hunched over. Jolly was starting to look his age. It made Rowan wonder what else was going on in the community to cause such a striking change in the once tireless leader.

"Justin is doing great from what I hear. Although I haven't seen him lately," Jolly answered her slowly, measuring each word as he spoke it.

She shook her head, not surprised with his evasive answer. They had been playing this game for a long time now.

Rowan decided on a new tactic. "Jolly, what's wrong? You look like crap and you sound worse."

A genuine smile broke out on his face and he laughed. "About time, too," he muttered almost to himself. "To be honest, Rowan, I need my queen. I can't do this alone anymore. These people here, they need a leader — a role model. You think Storm is that role model? Jewel? God forbid. You, Rowan. They need you," he said, watching her.

"You need me? Why me? Why has it always been me?" she begged for answers. She needed to understand this obsession of his. She needed to know why she had been chosen when so many others would gladly take her place.

"It is your destiny," Jolly spoke plainly, as if it was the most obvious answer in the world.

Once again Rowan was faced with trying to make sense of his circular ramblings. Her mind, which had momentarily cleared, clouded with his answer, "And you are to be my king?"

Jolly stood up and walked toward her. "No king, Rowan. It's too late for that. They need a leader they can relate to. I'm old, you're young and beautiful." He slipped his hand behind her neck, caressing her face with his thumb. "So beautiful. From the beginning, I knew."

Rowan could hardly take in his words while his hands were on her body. She began to tremble and felt her eyes pool with tears. He gripped her harder, holding her close to him.

"I am not your king. You are here for them, to fulfill your destiny, not to sleep with me, you dirty little child," he spat the words out in her face, his anger erupting suddenly.

She pulled herself together, blinking back the tears.

"Of course," she told him before her tears spilled down.

He let her go and stepped back, "Look at me. Do I look like a man who could hurt you? Do I look like a man who would take advantage of a person?"

He was full of rage, yelling at her.

She shook her head desperately, although the fear crawled up her body, closing her throat.

"Do you think I want to give up my leadership role to you? I do not, I'll tell you. This is not my idea. I can't help what they tell me to do. You are their next leader. I am simply fulfilling my own destiny and protecting my flock." Jolly's rage was all consuming, his body shaking and his face contorted.

"Of course," Rowan muttered.

"Already, it has begun," he said, collapsing into himself, quieting down. "You are collecting your energy, and look at me. I can't even control my own." He broke into sobs and fell to the floor.

Rowan was shocked! Never in her life had she seen anything like this. She threw herself to the floor and wrapped her arms around him. His body was wracked with sobs and he was shaking back and forth.

"It's okay Jolly. I'm here. It's okay," she soothed him, not knowing what else to do.

He looked up into her eyes; his were red with the tears streaming down his cheeks. "Do you see now? Do you see why you are needed here? I need you. They need you." He buried his head in her shoulders and continued to sob.

Rowan stroked his hair and held him. The man was falling apart in her arms and she was going to have to pick up the pieces.

• • •

Scratching his beard, Shane sat and watched the scenery fly by from his seat. Taking the Greyhound had been a hard choice, but he wanted to make this as real as he could. He needed to look, smell, and feel like he had been on the road for a while. The hair on his face from the last few days bothered him, but again, he wanted to really look the part.

His hair was longer than he liked it, too. That was just a lucky coincidence; he had missed his last hair appointment. He usually liked it short and spiky and never had a beard in his life. Sure, he had sported a five o' clock shadow, but never the five-day look. He hoped it would stop growing soon.

He'd been on the road for three days now and really needed a shower. He'd packed one backpack with a change of jeans, a few shirts, some underwear and socks and a notebook. Justin told him about the drifters that had shown up over the years, some had stayed and some had left, but they all seemed to have a few things in common: A backpack, an artist's journal, dirty clothes, and that lost look in their eyes. They'd all been wonderers seeking answers.

Justin warned him that not everyone there started that way, but it was a good way in. The cult was filled with all walks of life, rich and poor, over-educated and dropouts, religious and atheists, and everything in between. Some were seeking the occult while others had their own Catholic services on Sundays; some had never left the compound, having been born on site, while others still worked with the locals from the nearby town.

That was part of the allure to join such a group. Proof that utopia existed. If these people, all so different, could exist in a cohesive group, then there was hope for the world. They were the new leaders of the world: as soon as enough people saw how they lived, the rest of the world would follow.

Shane was headed to the high deserts of Arizona. The land was barren and the people left well enough alone. It was a culture born from survival in the elements, and most people out there figured if you were there you'd proved yourself worthy enough to stay. No matter what your strangeness was, survival gained respect. Jolly and his people had been on the compound for over thirty years.

Sitting back, he closed his eyes. He had about two more hours to go but try as he might, he couldn't get his body to relax. At some point, he was going to need to sleep, but that wasn't going to happen on this bus. Listening to the engine, he thought of Rowan. He hoped she was alright, wherever she was. And most of all, he hoped like hell she hadn't given up on him.

~

The air was dry and the afternoon sun prickled his skin as he stepped off the bus. He wanted nothing more than to shave his face to be rid of the dust and heat that seemed to collect there. He truly was in the middle of nowhere. Wickenburg was the closest town he could find to the compound and the way Shane saw it, town was stretching it. He had quite a walk to go. They truly were alone out here.

Checking his map one more time before hitting the road, he set out. The sun was high in the sky, but the temperature was not soaring along with it. In fact, it was almost pleasant. He had discovered that the nights were much colder than the days this time of year.

After walking for a few hours, he stopped at a roadside stand and ordered a sandwich. He was itching to check his map again, but didn't want to draw attention to himself.

"Where you walking to?" The man behind the counter asked him.

"Just walking, sir. Just walking," Shane answered evasively.

"Ha! You sound just like those hippy freaks. I'll tell you what. A grown man just walking with no life to get to. What has this world come to?" he grumbled as he prepared the sandwich.

Shane wanted to know about the hippies he referred to. "Should I be worried?"

"Damn straight, Son. You need to get a job, find a woman and settle down." The man almost yelled at him.

"No, I meant about the hippies. Should I be worried about them?" Shane bit down on a smile. He liked this guy.

"Naw. They seem harmless. But they all have names like Pancake and Moon Dust. They run around barefoot and drag their dirty kids with them. No schooling, no respect. Those kids won't even look me in the eye when I'm talking to them." The old man handed him his sandwich when his rant was over.

Shane took it gratefully and nodded his thanks, making sure to look him right in the eye. He might need an ally and this man seemed to have a good head on his shoulders. He took a bite and groaned with appreciation. The old man grunted back to him and went back to his work.

He knew he was close, but he needed to run into these people by accident. Maybe he should have stayed in town and waited for one of them to find him. Anxious to get there, he had just gotten off the bus and had started walking. Now he slowed his chewing, trying to figure out the best way forward.

When he finished he went to the old man. "Do you know of any places around here to spend the night?"

The old man looked at him hard. "Young man, I don't know what you're running from, but around here there's nothing but me, a few ranches, and Jolly's compound. This ain't no city, no hotels or youth hostels like you young people like. Your best bet is to head back the way you came," he scolded Shane and clucked his tongue.

"Thank you, sir. The food was excellent." With that, Shane walked out, heading toward the compound.

He walked for another half hour or so before a car whizzed past him blowing up dust. Shane covered his eyes and mouth hoping the dust would settle, but the car came to a screeching halt then started to back up. He watched it, hands still shielding his eyes, his stomach in knots.

"Hey stranger!" A young woman called over to him. "Whatcha doing in these parts?"

"Just walking," Shane answered her, smiling, pulling out the charm.

"Oh. You're cute. You got a place to stay, hon? Cause as soon as that sun goes down, this desert is gonna get real cold. There ain't nothing around here like a motel for miles." Her long blond hair looked like it hadn't been brushed in days.

She was young looking, but her demeanor seemed older, throwing Shane off a little. He usually could read people pretty well, but from where he stood, he couldn't really get a handle on who he was talking to.

"You offering?" he asked.

"It may not be my place, but yeah. If you stay out here in November, it can get pretty cold. And unless you have a big coat or some other magic in that sack of yours, you're going to freeze your ass off. Get in." She leaned back and gestured for him to get in the car.

Shane didn't hesitate. She fit the part: wild hair, young, friendly, and here. Even if she wasn't taking him to the compound, she could get him one step closer. He had nothing to lose at this point.

Jumping in the old box of a car, he settled in and reached for his seatbelt but found nothing there.

"Oh, you won't find that there. This is just a town car, we don't have seatbelts in them, they just got tangled up and gross, so we cut them out." She laughed as she watched him struggle.

"We?"

"Whoever's in charge. Over the years that's just how it's been done. I'm Star, by the way. What's your name?"

"Shane. Nice to meet you, Star. That is an interesting name."

"Thanks, it's short for Starlight," she told him and then turned her attention to the road as if that explained it all.

They drove in silence, bouncing down the road,

kicking up dust a mile behind them. There was nothing out here but small, dusty plants and dirt. Shane could hardly believe this was a road at all. How did people live out here? He watched for signs of a compound, but as far as he could see, he saw nothing.

Finally, Star slowed the old Nissan and turned onto an even smaller road. The road dipped and turned and started to climb a hill. At the top of the hill Shane had to bite his tongue to not shout in victory. Spread before him was the compound. Small buildings scattered the land with a few larger ones centered in the middle. Shane could see a few barns and what looked like a storage shed, maybe one large rounded building, too.

"Whoa! Star. Is this where you live?" Shane wanted to sound surprised.

She laughed at him and kept driving. She wound down a driveway and parked in front of one of the buildings.

Turning toward him, she smiled. "Yeah. We all live here. But don't worry, you're welcome here too. Everyone is. Come on, I'll introduce you around." She climbed out of the car.

Not wanting to waste any time, Shane bolted from the car, swinging his backpack over his shoulder. He followed his new friend as she made her way into one of the buildings. They walked through a small gate into a beautiful courtyard, with flowering vines wrapped around a large trellis and benches set amongst the pebbles in between two paved pathways. There were connecting rooms off each side, but they walked straight through to a large door. Once inside, Shane found himself in a large kitchen.

"Come on. Let's go find Eden," Star told him when he stopped to look around.

He fell in step with her as she walked through the

kitchen into a large dining room. The table was a long T-shape and looked as if it would sit twenty-five people, maybe more. They passed through the dining room into a large room with several couches and a game board set up in one corner.

The house was large but empty, and spotless. Shane didn't hear any voices or any other evidence of people. He followed her as she walked through the living room into a long hallway off to the right. After passing at least ten closed doors, she knocked on one at the end of the hall.

"Come in," a female voice called from inside.

Star gave Shane a reassuring smile and opened the door.

"Hi, Eden. I have a surprise for you," Star said as she bounded in the door. Shane couldn't hold back his own surprise at her wording. He was starting to feel like he was Christmas dinner or something.

Walking into the room, he took in his surroundings. It was a simple bedroom, white walls and picture window with a double bed in the corner, a desk and a lounge chair placed nicely near the light. Simple and clean, very much like how Rowan lived in her apartment. Shane shuddered.

"Hello," Eden's voice broke through Shane's thoughts.

He looked over at her and locked eyes with an older woman with long, dark hair and penetrating blue eyes. Her eyes seemed familiar, but he couldn't place them. Some people just have that look about them.

Shane drew himself up and extended his hand. "Hi, I'm Shane. Star offered me a room for the night. I guess it gets real cold up here at night."

The older woman looked him over as she slowly took his hand and shook it lightly. "Yes, our Star is often picking up strays and caring for them. One of the reasons she goes to town as much as she does."

A shiver fought its way out of Shane's spine. What an odd thing to say? On high alert, he repressed the shiver and smiled instead. "Well, I guess I'm the lucky one today."

"So, Shane. Why don't you sit and tell me about yourself." Eden gestured to the chair next to the bed. "Thank you, Star. You can get back to work now. I'm sure you'll see Shane again at dinner."

Star smiled at him one last time before bouncing out of the room.

"She's a sweet girl. But she should really be more careful picking up strangers on the side of the road," Shane started as he sat in the chair, placing his pack near his feet.

"Really? And you think that's dangerous?" Eden asked him.

"It can be. I just thought, as her mother, you might guide her out of that practice." Shane chose his words carefully, her relentless stare making him uncomfortable.

Eden laughed, "Oh, I'm not her mother."

"I'm sorry. I just figured you were."

"No need to apologize. In a way, I'm everyone's mother. But let's not waste our energy on Star, tell me about yourself."

Shane launched into the cover story he and Justin worked out. They talked for what seemed like an hour before Eden finally stood up and invited him to dinner. He would be assigned quarters after dinner and until then he should feel free to enjoy the property.

Shane walked out with a mixed sense of victory and dread. But for now, he would scope out the property and see if he could catch a glimpse of Rowan.

CHAPTER SIX

Fresh air was exactly what she had needed. Stepping outside for the first time in what might be several weeks felt magical. The desert air was dry with a hint of the coming winter, yet the sun warmed her skin. At first she didn't believe it when Cheri told her they were going for a walk, but then both doors were left open and Cheri stood just outside, waiting.

Learning to never question her good fortune, Rowan didn't ask where they were going or how long they would be out. She just lifted her face to the sun and felt her body start to thaw. Gradually her bones felt less heavy and her steps became lighter.

"Do I have you to thank for this?" Rowan asked her companion.

"You are in charge of your own destiny. I am simply here to assist you in finding your way," Cheri answered in her usual airy way.

Rowan snorted. She could still remember Cheri as a huffy adolescent. Cheri and Talia used to pal around together when they were younger, laughing at the crazy adults around them. Ironic that now she was one of the craziest here.

"And you believe that? That I'm the one in charge?"

Cheri stopped and turned to look right in her eyes. The other woman's were soft and full of pity, something Rowan was not expecting.

"Do you believe that? Not everyone here blindly follows; we all follow, but not all of us are blind. Do you see your son? Do you think if he was here he would have left you alone for so long? You have choices. I made my choice a long time ago. You are still struggling with yours, but that doesn't mean you're not in charge of your own life. Don't be blind, Rowan."

Cheri turned and started walking again. Rowan had to fight to keep standing, the surge of adrenaline that had flooded her system with the mention of Justin almost buckling her. Her mind temporarily frozen, she couldn't move.

"Come on." Cheri motioned for her to keep walking, back to her serene self.

Falling in step with her, Rowan desperately tried to keep her body calm. This gift was not given without risk. She needed to look like she was just strolling down the road enjoying her first taste of sunshine in weeks. Her mind was racing. Justin wasn't here? They didn't have him? He was safe, still living his life, she hadn't gone back on her promise to him.

Relief poured through her. For a full minute she was elated, before anger followed its path. *Those bastards!* She grimaced with the thought. After a few steps she had to chuckle at herself. Even if she knew they were lying, she would have come willingly, just in case. She would do anything to protect her son.

If she stayed they would leave him alone. If she took a leadership position, she would have power to ensure that they never bothered Justin or Talia again. She could accede to Jolly and protect her friends that were still here, the children, Lina. If she agreed to Jolly's plan, she could make everyone happy, be the protector within.

Forcing her face back up to the sky to keep up appearances, she smiled. Benevolence washed over her as Justin's security sank in. For the first time in a while she felt fire in her belly. She could do this. She could sacrifice her own life for those around her, for her family. Sweeping her arms up she leaned back, letting her new life plan solidify in her mind. It came to her in a flash. Jolly was right: This was her destiny, her place in the world, her life's work.

Straightening back up, she looked at Cheri, "Thank you for this walk. It has been very enlightening. If you ever need anything from me, just ask."

Cheri looked at her and tilted her head in confusion. After a few seconds, she nodded her head and they continued on their way. Rowan took the opportunity to reacquaint herself with the property. She could see the Instructary where she used to live and the Big House off in the distance, the offices, the barn and the Arena much closer. She figured out that she was in a new building, built away from the rest of the living quarters and much closer to the Arena. No wonder it didn't seem familiar. It hadn't existed before. She wondered what the larger plan had been in building it.

Children's laughter started to float up from the play area. Rowan smiled once again, turning to head down the path that lead to her old school. From the path she could see the children playing; there weren't very many of them. Before she left, there had been so many kids there was barely enough room to house them all, now the playyard looked huge as the few children scattered across the equipment.

Scanning the yard, her eyes found Lina. She looked

beautiful as always, her long, blonde hair flowing around her in the wind. She watched as the younger children darted back and forth, showing what treasures they found in the dirt. Lina would kneel down and admire each one before sending them back for more.

The entire scene brought back memories of years in that yard. Each and every fight at the Big House for equipment, books, supplies. She had built that school with Lina. Now she watched her friend stand alone protecting her own flock. Suddenly she understood why leaving was never an option for Lina. While Rowan left to protect her own child, Lina stayed to protect the rest.

As if she sensed her, Lina looked up. Frozen at first, she just stared, then started waving her hands like a crazy person. Without thinking, or asking, Rowan took off down the path, straight into her arms.

"Rowan! What are you doing here?" Lina squealed in her ear.

"They took me," she whispered quietly. "I've come back! I missed you all too much," she said loudly, for anyone listening.

Cheri came up behind them.

"Oh, my God! I can't believe you're here! Are you teaching again? Please say yes."

"No, Rowena is not teaching now," Cheri spoke in soft tones, such a dramatic contrast to Lina's excitement. "Jolly has other plans for her."

Lina pulled back from her hug and stared at Cheri. They had a silent exchange and then Lina's eyes landed on Rowan. "Will I see you?"

A maelstrom of emotions gripped her; afraid to speak, she nodded her head. Cheri pulled her back toward the path. She followed silently, completely overwhelmed. She wanted to stay, join Lina, go back to teaching, but knew that even if she stayed willingly, things would never be the same. She was not the same. The entire way back she kept asking herself the same question: could she do this to protect Justin? Would the hole Shane left in her heart be filled here? Could she stay and protect Lina, the children, from within? Would it be worth it—giving up on ever seeing Shane again? Was escaping even a possibility?

• • •

Walking into the dining room with Star, Shane didn't know what to expect. He had been told that everyone ate together every night so he hoped to see Rowan, but he hadn't gotten a whiff that she was even there.

Star had told him that they ate in silence and he should follow her lead. She did mention that some people liked to practice their natural voice before dinner but he could just observe for tonight. He heard what sounded like people humming when he approached the door.

Stopping short, Star had to nudge him a little to get him in the room. There were people all over the room singing and failing their arms over their heads. Singing wasn't even the right word, they were humming or chanting or yodeling. Maybe something like an om from a yoga class. About twenty people filled the room, some milling about, others standing behind their chairs at the table. Shane wondered if he was standing in the same room with Jewel or Colt and felt his muscles tighten.

Shaking it off, he glanced at Star in question, but she just smiled and boomed out a deep om herself. These people were crazy, or at least they looked crazy. Finally, after about ten minutes, an older woman at the far end of the table picked up her plate and moved through the buffet style set up, filling her plate. Slowly, while still making that god-awful noise, people followed her lead.

Star handed Shane a plate and he followed her to the food line, his stomach in a large knot. He had enough time to scan the room repeatedly looking for Rowan. After looking at every face at least twice, he knew she wasn't coming to dinner. Feeling too disheartened to look at anyone, he kept his eyes cast down and crept forward with the line. The food looked surprisingly delicious. A large platter of pork chops greeted him first, followed by a monster size bowl of mashed potatoes. Cooked carrots were next and a green salad sat at the end of the line.

Having filled his plate, he followed his host back to the table and she indicated the place next to her. Setting down his full plate, he waited. When everyone had gone through the line they all sat at once, silence filling the room. Shane had no idea who or what had triggered the group to sit, but it seemed as if they all knew to stop their noise making and sit on cue.

The only sounds in the room now were forks and knives scrapping across plates, people chewing and drinking. Shane watched, fascinated by the hand gesturing people did to ask for water jugs or salt and pepper. He would have thought with the silence that the people would be serious or tense, but with each small communication, people smiled to each other and went back to their food.

Feeling as if he was in some new age silent film, Shane gestured to the young man on his right for some water. The man handed it to him, smiled kindly, and went back to his food. It was all surreal; Shane felt like he was floating.

After about five minutes or so, three people jumped up and started clearing plates. Shane was far from done, so he started shoving food in his mouth as quickly as he could. How can people eat so fast? Just as he put down his last forkful, someone whisked his plate away. Still chewing, he reached for his napkin and wiped his face.

The room fell still and Shane could sense that something was about to happen. He waited. Just when he was starting to get really uncomfortable, the three people that cleared the plates burst into the dining room in make-shift costumes.

"Oh my! What should we do?" one of them shouted in an exaggerated way.

"I don't know. We should just call Jolly and have him fix it!" another spoke in a dopey voice.

"Oh no! What will Storm say?" the first one shouted to the diners.

"No. No. No. We need to solve this problem ourselves!" said the third, sounding a lot like Mickey Mouse.

Shane sat riveted to his chair. What the hell was going on? These people were putting on a crude play in the middle of dinner. He glanced around at his tablemates. Not all of them were enjoying the show, some even looked bored! Was this customary?

The play in front of him continued, but he couldn't really follow it. The three of them seemed to discussing the merits of figuring out a problem or getting help.

"That's it!" they all shouted at once, "Using your brain for more than masturbation!"

The three actors froze on their makeshift stage.

Shane started to clap, but noticed no one else moving, so he sheepishly put his hands down and watched the thespians file out into the kitchen area.

What the hell was that? Looking around, he saw that people were gesturing for the black and white coffee thermos on the table. Shane waited, having no idea what would happen next.

An anonymous hand placed a plate of some kind of pie in front of him and he didn't hesitate to start eating it. It wasn't good, but not knowing when it would disappear, he ate it all.

"Any comments and observations this evening?" a female voice spoke from the far end of the table.

For a long moment, no one spoke.

"I have an observation," a young woman said, "I observed myself today getting really angry when I discovered that someone took my jacket out of the office suites. I really liked that jacket and someone just took it. I felt violated. I guess I was really attached to it."

"Nice observation," was repeated over and over again from the different people around the table. They sounded like robots to Shane, but he was still a little shell-shocked from that play.

And so the evening went. People spoke up and made small comments about their day, or observations about themselves and the table would mutter back 'thank you for the comment' or 'nice observation'. Shane glanced at his watch. Dinner had started a little over two hours ago and he was ready for these shenanigans to be over.

Finally, the table fell quiet. No one spoke for at least three minutes. The same woman who had started off the food line got up and walked out of the room. People started filing out one by one. The group started chattering and it looked as if a clean-up crew had formed to clear the rest of the dishes from the table.

Shane looked at Star. He still had no idea where he was sleeping and after that experience, he really needed to be in a quiet place alone. She grabbed his hand and led him back the same way they'd come earlier when he met Eden.

"So, that was dinner," she said breathlessly. "What'd ya think?"

Shane weighted his words carefully. "That was an interesting experience."

She laughed and kissed him on the check. "This is you. Night."

She left him in front of a door near Eden's room. He slowly opened it and sighed with relief when he saw a single bed and a small dresser in the corner. He had his own room. Thank God.

CHAPTER SEVEN

Amazing what can happen in a week. Rowan now had a new room with windows, a balcony, a bathroom, and doors that opened and shut at her own hand. She even had a key so she could control who came and went. She was allowed to go to dinners, not with the entire group yet, of course, but still, it was nice to see people again.

Jewel was the only one who seemed less than pleased to see her back. If Jewel only knew how Rowan really felt about her own imprisonment—they had so much more in common than she would ever know.

So far, the only real work she'd been allowed to do was during the intruder drill. Most of the property went into hiding, but a select few had to fight and Jewel made sure that Rowan had a front and center seat for that. Before, Rowan had always hated violence, but now that she no longer had a child here, she found it much more tolerable.

It had seemed Jewel was disappointed with her nonplused reaction to the drill. Apparently, Jewel wasn't ready to give up her hatred just yet, but Rowan just didn't have the strength to hate her anymore. She was not in love with Colt, she didn't have a son to protect; she simply had herself. Rowan was finding it increasingly easy to keep her emotions in check when it was only her own soul on the line.

"Good morning!" Cheri called out to her as she walked in.

Rowan turned and greeted her, "Morning."

Cheri stopped and stared at her, "I see you found the clothes in your closet."

Rowan grimaced. This morning when she got dressed she discovered that all of her jeans and shirts had been taken and in their place were long flowing skirts and dresses with silk wraps. Her clothes were now all soft cotton and silk or bamboo. Jolly was getting her to look the part.

Rowan held in a giggle. She felt ridiculous but would never admit that out loud. Cheri just shook her head and dropped the subject.

"You have a busy day. Jolly is on his way over and Jewel and Colt need a meeting with you after that."

The last part caught her attention. "Really? Jewel and Colt want a meeting with me. This morning?"

"That's what's on your schedule."

"I have a schedule?" Rowan couldn't hide the astonishment in her voice.

Cheri stopped cleaning her room and looked right at her. "Well Ro, looks like you made your choice."

Rowan's stomach felt like it collapsed into itself. She braced herself against the desk and nodded her head. She hoped like hell it was the right one.

~

"Sweet, sweet Rowena, you look perfect. It's so nice to finally see you where you belong." Jolly's voice slid along her veins, irritating her to no end while he fussed with her new tie-dyed, psychedelic clothing. She felt as if she was a doll he was playing with.

Rowan smiled through gritted teeth, but held her tongue. Jolly's touch made her skin crawl. She didn't want his hands on her, anywhere. She didn't want his smiles or his compliments. She wanted him out of her room. This was going to be a lot harder than she'd thought.

"You will do so much good here. These people, they need you. They need your beauty, your spirit, your vitality." Jolly spoke to her as if he was speaking to a full auditorium.

He may be evil, but he did speak the truth—in a warped way. These people were taking her life and her spirit; whether they needed it was still debatable.

"Tonight you will make your grand entrance. They will love you." Jolly stood back admiring his work.

Rowan felt like a class one idiot. She was wearing a flowing wrap-around dress with a long silk scarf. Had she been over six feet tall, she might have been able to pull it off, but her 5 foot 3 frame was swallowed in the yards of fabric. She turned to face the mirror. It was so much worse than it felt. All she could see was an ocean of tie-dyed blue, purple, and green swirling around her from head to toe. The only body part visible was her face with her too big eyes peering out from under the weight of the cloth. She looked like she was seven years old again.

"Great!" Rowan squeaked. "I can't wait."

Jolly was in her face before she even took her next breath. He pushed her against the wall, wrapping his fingers around her throat, squeezing slowly.

"Make no mistake. I will not tolerate your negativity. You have a lot of work to do still, but you had better get a handle on that smart mouth of yours quick," he growled at her.

Rowan would have laughed had she not been on the verge of blacking out from lack of oxygen. This was the Jolly she knew. This was the Jolly she refused at eighteen. This was the Jolly she ran from.

She nodded her head and the pressure around her throat eased, slightly. Just as she gasped in her first breath he clamped down again.

"Don't play games with me, girl. I know everything about you and I will destroy you." He glared at her for an extra few seconds and then finally let go.

She doubled over, the dreaded fabric falling into her face, smothering her again. Yanking the scarf off, she pulled in several deep breaths, causing her head to spin. Knowing what would happen if she passed out, she willed her heart to slow down and her breathing to even out. By the time she stood, Jolly was gone.

• • •

The week had been one shock to the system after another. Each morning started with a morning meeting where everyone announced to the group what tasks they would accomplish that day. He had been to group meditation twice, three self defense classes, participated in an intruder alert drill, and more than his fair share of crazy dinners. Each night seemed to have some sort of theme to it. One night they read a story and people came dressed as their favorite character. Another night they read a bizarre folk tale and had a lively discussion at dinner about the morals and lessons they learned.

Shane had been placed on a work crew, which meant that most days he worked four hours in the morning on clearing fields before breaking for lunch, and then four more hours on a construction project.

After several long days here, he hadn't laid eyes on Rowan. Nor had he met this infamous Jolly or even Jewel or Colt.

He heard that Jewel was the one who set up the intruder drill, but she never appeared. It seemed as if the group was split into two or maybe even more. He hadn't seen Lina either, but did walk by what looked like a school and wondered if that was the nursery Rowan had lived in. There were no kids at the meals, the mediations, or at the work crews.

It was time for him to up his game. He needed to start asking questions and poking around. He needed to make sure Rowan was really here and he wasn't just wasting his time.

"Did you hear the news?" Fern asked him as they walked to their job site after lunch.

"Nope."

"Jolly and all his people are coming to dinner tonight. He says he has a big surprise for all of us." Fern spoke excitedly. He was a fairly young man with big teeth and dark red hair. When Shane first met him, he wrote him off as kind of slow, but after spending the week together, he learned that Fern wasn't slow at all, just very quiet and highly observant.

"A big surprise, huh? Any idea what that could be?" Shane asked.

"I got a few ideas, yeah. He used to eat with us all the time, ya know. Everyone ate together, but then last year or so they've been sharing their own meals and meetings."

"And you think that's not good?" Shane knew he was pushing him, but he needed to find out just how much things had changed over the last few years. How crazy Jolly had gotten over this Rowan thing.

Fern paused and looked up at the sky, "I think

living in a group means you live in the group. I get that the teachers live with the kids and all, but Jewel and Jolly and them all? I think they need to live in the group like the rest of us."

"Seems fair. What do you think this surprise is?"

"Oh, Jolly's got some big plan that's going to make us all real happy and looks like he's ready to roll it out tonight." Fern smiled at him, his green eyes shining with the possibilities.

Shane's gut tightened; Jolly's big plan involved stealing a life. He smiled through his agitation and nodded his head in agreement with Fern. Like the rest of them, he would have to wait until tonight. But he knew. Somehow, he was sure that tonight he would finally see Rowan.

~

Dinner was early that evening. It was a rushed affair with no play or dessert. After the plates were cleared away Lisa, Shane now knew her name, stood, and everyone filed out of the dining room after her. Shane had learned that Lisa was a leader of sorts, but of what other than pacing the dinners he wasn't sure. There were so many people here and everyone seemed to have various jobs and schedules. Shane was trying to learn them all, but knew he wasn't allowed to know about most of what went on around him.

As the group walked, in silence, Star took his hand in hers and they continued to walk together. Awkward at first, but within a few steps he felt his arm relax in her hand. Shane desperately wanted to ask where they were going and why, but he bit his tongue and followed the silent people in front of him. Star smiled reassuringly while squeezing his hand. He knew he was way too tense and it was probably starting to show.

Moving his neck side to side, he forced his shoulders to relax and tried to get his leg muscles to calm down. As with the rest of him, they were coiled and ready to strike. He was talking himself off the ledge when Star surprised him by dropping his hand and bringing both her hands on his shoulders, giving him a massage while they walked.

His first instinct was to pull away, but her hands gripped him tightly, not letting him go. Remembering his undercover role, he let her have her way with her hands and felt his body relax even more. Looking up, he realized they were walking into the Arena. Star continued her massage while steering him over to the side, placing him just in front of her.

He sat down and felt her knees press into his sides as she sat just behind him. Now that they were sitting, her hands were even more effective. *Oh, that felt really good*—it had been a long time since anyone had touched him, let alone massage his aching muscles. For a moment, he forgot all about where he was and why he was there. He closed his eyes and dropped his head, giving Star free reign.

After a few minutes, the tension in the Arena changed. Opening his eyes, he looked up into the center of the stage. For a moment, his breath stopped. There was Rowan, standing on a makeshift stage, looking like a Goddess. She had on a long flowing dress and a long scarf wrapped tightly around her neck. All the tension flooded back into his body; his heart rate spiked and he knew he had a problem. Rowan was staring at him, hard. Her hazel eyes were glowing with disgust as she watched Star's hands on his body, her legs practically wrapped around his waist.

Shane sat up abruptly, almost knocking Star over. His eyes never left Rowan's. Oh yeah, Rowan was pissed, but there was a flash of fear that he caught too. What Shane didn't know was whether that fear was because another woman's hands were on him, or just because he was there.

• • •

The last thing Rowan expected to see was Shane. And to see Shane with Star's hands all over him was simply too much! Star, of course it was Star. She was young, beautiful, and easy. Jolly loved sending her to town because she always came back with a stray. How in the hell she found Shane was beyond comprehension.

She needed to think, to keep a clear head. She was about to be presented to these people. It wasn't as if she didn't know all of them, but she had been gone for years. The rumors and stories must be all over the place. Just more proof that Jolly had no idea what this place was really like. In her room, this seemed like a good idea. Jolly would be happy and he would leave Justin alone, but now, standing here in this ridiculous outfit in front of everyone, she was having serious second thoughts.

And Shane! What was he doing here? How did he even find this place?

"Hello, Lovers!" Jolly started. Rowan bit back her teeth — she hated that greeting. "We have gathered here tonight to welcome home a wonderful woman."

The entire Arena stilled. Rowan was almost afraid to breathe.

"Last time we saw her she was running our school, in charge of our most precious commodity — our future. Some of us remember when the sky opened up and blessed us with her presence. And some of us remember when she was a gawky teenager rebelling against the rules." He stopped and chuckled into the microphone.

There was a murmur of quiet laughter in the stands. Rowan fought the urge to snort and roll her eyes. Of course they laughed with him—even when they didn't even know why—he laughs, they laugh.

"Now, a few years ago she just poof, disappeared. A lot of you thought she fled, some of you thought she was booted out, and even more of you thought she was retraining. But I can tell you now that none of those things were true. Evil are the rumors that fly around this place and distract us from our most important work.

"No, my lovers. She wasn't fleeing, she didn't get the boot, and never would this angel need retraining. No, she was on a mission. A mission for you. I sent her out into the world for you. She sacrificed years for you and lived among the dirty, grungy, sleeping people of this world. All for you. Now she knows everything she needs to about the people we are all trying to save. Please welcome back Rowena Queena!" Jolly flung his hand in her direction and everyone stood and cheered as if she was some sports star.

Fighting hard to keep the laughter threatening to bubble up at bay, Rowan stepped up next to Jolly and waved. Looking out at the people, she wondered where everyone was. Before she left, the Arena almost felt full when they all gathered, but now barely a quarter of the seats were filled. She looked around for her friends. For Lina and the kids. Sure enough, they were all there, off to the side. Lina was smiling along with the rest of them, but when they locked eyes Lina raised her eyebrow questioningly at her.

Yes, she would have some explaining to do. But right now, she just needed to get through this and get back to the sanctuary of her room. Unfortunately, Jolly had other plans. He thrust the microphone in her hands and stepped back. Rowan froze—she was expected to speak.

When the noise died down and everyone sat back down, she brought the microphone to her lips.

"H-Hi," she stammered. "I'm a little overwhelmed with your reception. Thank you." She laughed a little to gather her thoughts. With a deep breath, she plowed forward. "It feels so good to be back! I can't wait to get back to work."

Nothing else would come out of her mouth. She couldn't utter another lie. These were her friends, her family, how could she stand up here and lie to them about her so-called mission?

"Traveler's report!" Someone shouted from the stands.

She was ready for that one, bringing the microphone back up, she smiled at the voice. "Who was that? Fern? No, Rio?"

"Rio!"

"Rio! I have been traveling for years and we have young children with us tonight, none of us want to sit that long for my full report. But what I can tell you is that the world is vast with infinite possibilities. You just never know what could happen next. Change is the only constant."

With that, Rowan handed the mic back to Jolly and stepped back. She didn't know what else Jolly had planned for the evening, but she knew she was done. She walked back the way she came, hoping that Cheri would be there to help her back to her room.

When she got to the tunnel no one was there so she

just kept walking. The scarf wrapped around her neck was starting to suffocate her. Reaching up to loosen it, she remembered the bruises it was hiding and left it. She could hear Jolly's voice but couldn't make out what he was saying. Seeing Shane had thrown her. What was he doing out there? How long has he been here? Why now? And to have Star's hands on him, he'd been all too happy about that until he looked up. Had Star already slept with him? Would Shane do that?

She stopped short and almost growled at the thought. She knew she was alone — finally. With a fleeting thought she wondered if she could run. Run from everything — from Shane, from Star, from Jolly, from her own mind. Would she run far enough this time, fast enough? Did that even exist? Was there a place on earth that was far enough away from Jolly that he wouldn't find her, wouldn't threaten her? Wouldn't steal her back and lock her in a room?

She didn't veer off course. Touching the tender marks on her neck, she walked a straight line from the Arena to her room. Her last thoughts before locking her door and slipping into bed were of Shane. She needed to figure out why he was here and how to get him out.

CHAPTER EIGHT

Shane held his breath as he watched her walk away. Never turning around, never slowing down, she just marched off the stage and disappeared into the back of the Arena. So that's how it's done around here, a lot of lies and manipulation. He wondered if these people really believed any of that theater performance. And 'Hello Lovers'? What the fuck was that? Did the guy not realize there were kids in the stands?

Jolly looked a lot different than he'd pictured. After everything he heard, he built up this image of what this big, bad cult leader looked like. But he had looked just like a regular guy. Sure, he had longish, wavy hair, but Shane saw how it was cut and styled purposefully. There was nothing unintentional about him. He looked very much like your average Joe, with bright blue eyes, jeans, boots, and a work shirt with the sleeves rolled up. No beard, no creepy glasses, nothing that would set him apart from anyone else here.

His voice, on the other hand, made it clear he was used to speaking to large groups. He may look like some guy about to give a presentation on tractor parts, but when he opened his mouth he transformed into a different person. His voice was deep and booming, commanding the Arena, transfixing his audience. Everyone but Shane, that was. He was still stunned at the entire affair — how did this seemingly normal guy take control of these people? What secrets did he promise them?

His skin was crawling. The whole evening was creepy. All these people sat riveted, listening to this crazy man rant on and on about nonsense. Meanwhile, Rowan was right there and then she was gone. Why did she agree to stand in front of these people and lie to them? Why wasn't she shouting from the roof tops that she was here under duress? What hold did this man have on these people?

He started to stand, hoping to leave, but Star pulled him back down. She squeezed his waist with her thighs and wrapped her arms around him. He didn't want to make a scene, but he needed to get out of there. The reason he was there had just raced off the stage and he was itching to go find her.

Star made it clear that he was to go nowhere. Even when he whispered that he really needed to go to the bathroom, she didn't let up. It looked like he was there for the duration. Over an hour later, Jolly put his head down and bowed to his audience. Thank Fuck! Shane was about to burst out of his skin.

As he stood up, he noticed the group of kids being shepherded out of the Arena. He had forgotten that they were even there; they had sat through the entire night without so much as a peep! Right there proof that something was wrong around here.

"Wow! That was—" he started to say to Star.

"I know, right. So exciting. Everyone thought she had run away, but I knew Rowena would never do that. She was supposed to marry Jolly, ya know. But then he changed his mind. Said as much as they loved each other, she had a greater purpose. Even Jolly has had to sacrifice love for The Work," she rushed her words together in a dreamy cadence.

Shane almost choked. How the fuck do these people really believe any of this crap? Shane listened to the conversations around them as they all walked back to the main house. Everyone was talking about the amazing sacrifice Jolly had made for them and how Rowan was going to make everything better. Shane felt sick by the time they arrived at the Big House.

"So, do you want to come back to my room tonight?" Star asked him, picking up his hand one more time.

Shane's head snapped up and all at once he felt like a complete ass. All night she had been touching him, massaging him, holding his hand, but he had been so wrapped up in Rowan he never thought about the implications. He needed to get his head in the game here or he was going to blow his cover.

"Um," he started and then pulled his shit together. "You know what, babe, as much fun as that sounds, I'd better not. We have a huge crew tomorrow and I'm still the new guy. I need to keep up with everyone. And if I go back with you, there's no way I'll have anything left in the morning." He smiled at her and leaned into her for good measure.

"All right, I guess. Don't be a stranger," she said, coyly.

He didn't watch her walk away, he turned and practically ran back to his room. Now that he knew for certain that Rowan was here, he was going after her right now.

~

Shane crept along the edge of the building listening

for people. It was late, but God damn if these people just didn't sleep. He'd had to wait a good hour before the clean-up crew was done and he could even get out of the house. Breaking into houses had been easier than sneaking out of the Big House. There were a lot of random buildings on site and people seemed to be everywhere. Seemed like every office building had at least one residents' quarters, or what Shane would call an apartment.

After searching a variety of office type buildings and discovering apartments, he headed up the hill to a newer looking set of buildings. These were all grouped together and far off, as if set apart on purpose. After cruising though the offices and finding no one, not even a hidden apartment, he made his way over to a well-lit, active building, spilling with people.

He had been searching the property for over three hours now, and was surprised to suddenly find so many people awake and milling about. These rooms seemed to be bigger than the ones near the main house and for some reason he was sure he would find Rowan here. Rounding the first corner, he heard voices.

"I'm not being defiant, I just don't entirely understand it all," a female voice said through the darkness.

"One doesn't need to understand to follow orders, Jewel," Jolly's voice sailed off just in front of where Shane was crouching.

He turned and snuck off the other way, hoping they were more interested in their argument than listening to the bushes shake right beside them. Scurrying along the wall, he listened to the noise. Music played, radio shows blared, and people talked loudly to each other. It sounded as if the people who lived in this building were having a party. He wondered if Rowan was up, partying with them. As if on cue he found one room that was completely dark and quiet. His gut squeezed and he knew — Rowan was in there.

Shane skirted the wall, looking for exterior doors, and almost laughed out loud when he found one. Opening it with ease, he snuck inside. There was a lot of commotion down the hall, but Shane walked toward the darkness. After circling around a couple of times just to be sure, he found the right door and used his makeshift tools to open it.

Slipping inside and relocking it, he waited, listening. After a few crucial seconds, he took a step into the room. A black mass came out of nowhere and jumped on his back, pushing him forward and covering his eyes and mouth.

"Rowan! It's me," he whisper-shouted to his attacker, hoping like hell it was Rowan attacking him and not someone else.

They lay on the floor, panting hard. He could feel her on top of him, trying to hold him down.

"It's me, baby," Shane tried again. This time her grip loosened from his face and she sat up.

"Are you fucking crazy?" she hissed at him, standing up.

"Nice to see you, too," he growled at her.

A light snapped on and Shane turned around to see Rowan in a pair of men's pajamas. She looked beautiful despite her too large eyes and her heaving chest. My God, how he missed her. She was too thin and looked wild with her hair askew and her eyes frantically darting around the room, but deep within his chest his heart cracked open just a sliver when he laid eyes are her.

"What are you doing here?" she asked, stepping away from him.

"I missed you, baby," he closed the distance between them and gathered her up in his arms. He didn't mean to, but he felt compelled to touch her, to breathe in her scent, to feel her skin. She felt so good in his arms, as if he could finally inhale.

She pushed him away, frantic. "Get away from me. You need to get the hell out of here. Make up a story now. Tell them your mother died, your brother is sick, you need to donate a kidney. Get out while you still can."

Rowan sounded hysterical and her voice was rising. Shane worried about being overheard so he backed up, giving her as much space as he could in the small room.

"Rowan. I'm not going anywhere without you. Justin told me how to get here and we both want you back."

Rowan froze when he dropped Justin's name. "Justin sent you? Is he okay?"

"He's fine, but he would be a lot better if you were back home where you belong."

She laughed, outright belly laughed at him. Wiping away the tears in her eyes, she muttered under her breath, "Where I belong."

Shane froze; this was not what he had hoped for. It's what he feared, all those nights lying awake in his bed, his heart in his throat, his stomach in knots — *the longer you take, the more time they have with her. Please, let it not be too late!*

"Let's go. I can get us out of here. We have plenty of time, it's only just after one in the morning. I can get us to the main road and we can hitch a ride. There's a guy at the gas station who will help us."

She just looked at him. "Are you that naïve? You really think if we could walk out of here and get help from Mr. Wilson any of us would still be here through our adolescence?"

Shane's eyes went wide. Yeah, he fell for that one. *Damn it.*

"Why are you doing this?"

"Doing what?" Rowan almost yelled at him. "Protecting my family? Ensuring Justin has a future away from this place? Keeping the monster close so I might one day have some control?"

It was when Rowan threw her hands in the air and looked up at them that Shane saw the bruises on her neck. His entire body coiled at once. What the hell happened to her? He could clearly see fingerprint bruises on each side of her neck as if someone tried to suffocate her.

Without thinking he stormed toward her, seeing red. "Who touched you? Who tried to kill you?" he roared.

Her hands flew to her neck. "It was nothing. No one tried to kill me, he was just making a point. I'm fine."

He gently caressed her neck, inspecting the damage while she stood stock still, every muscle tensed under his touch. They were fresh, which meant this happened while he was here, in the last day or so. Tears of frustration threatened to fall. "Oh baby. I'm so sorry. Please forgive me. I'm so sorry."

Her skin was so soft, so beautiful. He longed to hold her, to envelope her in his arms and protect her. He kissed every bruise gently, wishing he could heal her skin with his kisses. She stopped fighting him, relaxing her body into his and giving him access to her neck.

Before he knew it, he was kissing up her jawline in search of her mouth. When he finally found it, he thought he'd died and gone straight to heaven. His lips covered hers, his tongue asking for more. It wasn't until she kissed him back that he lost control. She opened her mouth and sucked his bottom lip. causing a rush of blood down south.

He groaned and rubbed his now throbbing cock against her. Seeing nothing, feeling everything, as if all his fear and self loathing instantly mutated into desire, he was suddenly a rage of sexual need. Her arms wrapped around his neck, holding him closer to her, her mouth devoured him. For months he had wondered if he would ever be able to taste her again. For months he had thought she was lost to him. Now she was here in his arms. Everything felt right, perfect, as it should be.

"Rowena, you still awake?" Jolly's voice through the door startled them both. Rowan's head jerked back as if Shane had burned her. She froze, terrified. "Rowena?" he called again. "No, she's not awake Jewel, we can talk to her in the morning."

They heard his voice trail away from the door. The bubble was popped and Rowan was backing away from him.

"You need to go," she hissed at him. "Please. Just leave right now. No one will notice if you leave now. Go back to Justin. Keep him safe."

"The fuck I'm leaving here without you."

They heard more footsteps outside her door. Rowan turned away from him and crawled back in bed, throwing the covers over her as if trying to hide. Shane stood watching her in silence for a few lonely moments before he reluctantly slid out one of the windows and made his way back to his room on the other side of the property.

If there was one thing he knew with every fiber of

his being, Rowan was not staying here and he was not leaving without her. He would not fail again.

~

Grasping the pick ax with both hands, Shane threw his back into the swing and hit the wall, tearing through the old wood. Anger simmered just under his skin, he was so close to her—he had touched her, kissed her, held her—yet here he was, still here and still without her. Having been assigned to this crew a couple of days ago, he was getting comfortable enough around his crewmates to throw himself into the work. It felt good to be this physical, to slam his pick ax against the side of the barn. Maybe he needed to start running again—to work out some of his frustration. He might be able to hold his shit together better the next time he saw Rowan. No wonder she pushed him away, he was completely out of control last night.

He had asked Fern about running trails, but the guy just looked at him blankly. Shane had been away from his regular exercise routine long enough and it was becoming painfully obvious that he needed to figure out how to get in some running time soon or he was going to regret it when he finally got home. With Rowan.

He hacked away at the old barn for a good thirty minutes before someone called break. Wiping the sweat from his forehead, he put down his ax and ambled over to the break area. Sometimes there were snacks or water. Sometimes not. So far he hadn't figured why.

Beck, Fern, and Skip were all on his crew. Skip seemed to be in charge which confused him because Beck had been the one to assign them all the task of tearing the old barn down in the first place. That sort of threw him at first, but Beck made it clear that first day that this was Skip's crew and he was in charge.

"How's it going, Shane? You gonna have that side ripped out by the end of the day?" Skip asked him as he grabbed a water.

"Maybe. Not sure yet."

"Maybe? What kind of answer is that?" Beck chimed in.

Shane's eyes widened in surprise, but he continued to drink the rest of his water. "It's the only reasonable answer there is right now. I don't know what surprises there are over there. Is that a problem?"

Beck laughed but then glared at him, "No, no problem. Just most people around here are straight up yes or no types."

Shane took a breath. He wanted to fit in and not piss people off, but this guy had been riding his ass for days now and he was sick of it. Add that to his worry about what was happening with Rowan and he had no bandwidth to deal with assholes right now.

"I could tell you yes but then look like a failure for not finishing it, or I could tell you no and you could ride my ass for being negative, so the way I figure it, the best and most honest answer is maybe," he spit out, glaring right back at Beck.

"Easy, Shane. Don't let him get to you. Beck, back off — go find someone else to mess with." Fern stepped in, guiding Shane away from the group, handing him a banana.

"Thanks."

"So Shane, have you seen Star lately?"

This threw him, "No. Why?"

"Well, you just seem a little tense and I know she usually helps."

All kinds of red flags were waving in the air with that one. Shane stopped and looked at Fern.

"Go on," he said.

"It's what she does. She's really good with new recruits, helps get them settled in and comfortable. And let's face it, sex is just a physical release anyway. Looks like you could use some."

"Let me get this straight, you're telling me that Star is here to help get the new people comfortable and part of that is having sex with them?" Shane was working hard not to punch him in the face. Never had he heard a man disrespect a woman so matter-of-factly.

Fern looked at him and sort of laughed, "Yeah! We've all done it at some point. Don't be afraid. We all get it. She's worried about you. You keep telling her that you'll come see her and you haven't."

Stalling to get his mind wrapped around what Fern was telling him, he drank more water. Was he for real? Star had slept with everyone here just for the physical release sex provided? Star and Fern talked about him, and now he was getting his chops busted because he hadn't slept with her yet?

Rowan was right, this place was fucked up with a big capital F. Was Star down with the way she was being treated here? Did she even know any better? If she grew up here, she might not. Torn between staying undercover and wanting to deck the guy, Shane swallowed his water and reeled in his anger.

"Good to know." Was all he could get out. Nothing more. He was so pissed, he couldn't even make small talk. With a tight smile, he nodded and turned back to the group.

Heading back, he noticed two women walking on the main road. He stopped and watched, recognizing Rowan. At least she wasn't in long, flowing robes this time. She was being followed. Rowan looked upset, her head down, marching down the road silently.

Fern startled him when he approached. "Now that is an untouchable."

"What?"

"Rowena Queena. Jolly's answer to everything wrong. She's been here her whole life and then bam, just disappeared one day. Rumors flew around, but Jolly promised us she would return. And low and behold, she did." Fern had an edge to his voice, unlike before.

"I take it you don't approve."

"It's not my place to approve. Maybe before she lived out there she could have been the answer, but now? I just don't know."

"The answer?" Shane asked, hungry for anything he could learn about her.

"That's the dirty little secret no one wants to talk about. She was poised to take over. Be our true leader. A real Jolly and Storm rolled into one. She became a master. Before she was twenty, she could get anything done. Started a school, changed the rules for the kids, divided the training, all kinds of stuff. And then just poof. She was gone."

Shane could barely move. The information flowing out of Fern was gold and he wanted more. But then Skip and Beck walked up.

"What's up?" Beck asked.

"Nothing," Shane started but Fern interrupted him.

"Look. It's Rowena and Cheri," Fern explained.

"I'm so excited she's here. She really will take us to the next level. We need that. Jolly told me himself, he can only do so much. We need her to propel us forward," Skip spoke with reverence.

"Don't you think it's strange that she left her son out there?" Beck asked.

"You mean Jolly's son? I think he's on a mission of his own. He'll be back. No way Jolly would leave him out there. Look at how awake she is. The way she walks. Wow, man." Skip watched the pair walk out of view.

Shane darn near choked. He saw that she was upset and deep in thought. He could almost hear her mind working a mile a minute from here, and this kid saw enlightenment. It really is all about the eye of the beholder, isn't it?

"Jolly's son?" Shane asked, prying further.

"That's the way I heard it. Of course, no one will admit that to anyone." Beck told him.

"No man, that's Romano's kid," Fern tried to correct him.

"Naw. That was just a front, because she was so young. But Jolly knew it was the right time." Beck kept talking as if he really had the inside scoop.

Shane raised an eyebrow at Fern in question. He just shrugged back, making Shane shake his head. These guys didn't know anything for sure, just years of stories. As always, the youngest ones with the least amount of real information spoke with highest conviction.

• • •

Her visit with Lina had been inspiring. The Instructary needed a lot of work. The roof leaked, the bathrooms needed maintenance, and the children needed new toys. Lina had spent a lot of her budget 'researching' curriculum, and the rest of the school had suffered. The guilt weighed heavily on Rowan knowing what her research trips were really about.

What she really needed was her clothes. The short

skirt was better than the long dress from last night, but she still didn't feel like herself. Of course, she hadn't felt like herself in weeks.

Waking up this morning, she had blamed everyone and everything for her fate. She had done everything the universe asked of her. She went willingly with Jewel, she stopped fighting Jolly, she accepted her place here, all to protect those she loved. And now Shane was here!

Somehow he had found his way here and straight into the arms of Star. She knew the name of that game; Shane would give in to her soon, otherwise he would be called out as over attached to the outside and banished. If the new recruits didn't start sleeping with someone here soon, they were accused of all kinds of things and the pressure would mount until they broke. Jolly's first step in their long road to freedom.

Her blood boiled. How the hell was she supposed to pull this off while Shane was here? There was no way she could play the role of the dedicated leader with Shane as one of her followers; it was bad enough trying to convince Lina — who had seen right through her thin layer of bullshit. Lina didn't buy it for a second. If she wasn't mistaken, she thought Cheri was having a hard time buying it herself.

"Good morning." A sharp knock on her door startled her.

"Give me ten minutes, I'll come out," she called to the door, not even caring who was outside wanting her.

She heard footsteps retreat and let out a long sigh. Marching over to her closet, she went through what was hanging there. Where were her regular clothes? What right did they have just coming in here and taking them? She couldn't wear any of this crap anymore. She'd keep the scarf until her bruises healed, but she wanted her jeans back.

"Cheri!" she called down the hall. "I need my clothes!"

She heard nothing and started walking down the hall looking for her. She had to be around here somewhere. As she opened doors looking for her, she got more and more fired up. She pounded on the locked doors calling Cheri's name. Most of the rooms were empty, but some looked like they had occupants in them. One of these had to be Cheri's room. Flinging another door open, she ran smack into Jolly in his night shirt.

"What the hell is all that fucking noise?" Jewel's voice startled her even more. Her eyes darted from Jolly, looking like a deranged Santa, to Jewel in bed, naked.

Rowan couldn't help it, she smacked her hand on her mouth, but not before laughter came flooding out of it. She turned on a dime and slammed the door shut. Barely breathing now, she continued her search for Cheri.

Much to her relief, Cheri turned down the hall with fresh towels.

"Cheri! I need my clothes," she barked at her, although the laughter did help to lighten her mood somewhat.

"You don't have any clothes?" Cheri looked at her, perplexed.

They started walking back to her room together. Rowan snorted. "Oh, I have clothes. I want my clothes. Where are they?"

Cheri nodded and smiled slightly. She handed her the towels and then turned back the other way.

By the time Rowan had placed her new towels in

her bathroom, Cheri was back with her box of clothes. Dressing in jeans and a long sleeve shirt, she brushed her short hair and wrapped a scarf over her bruises. Now that she felt more like herself, she was ready for the rest of the day.

Before she left they used to have a morning meeting, but things were very different now. It seemed as if the group was split into three parts. Jolly, Storm and few of their most loyal followers that never seemed to leave their sides all lived and worked here in this new building, while everyone else still met at the Big House. And she assumed the kids and teachers still lived in the Instructary.

She needed to talk to someone about the state of the Instructary and find out what was going on with the rest of the people. It was time to meet her people.

She found the common kitchen area and made coffee, figuring that someone would show up soon. It was almost noon, after all. About ten minutes later, Jolly walked in, all smiles. Rowan watched him, but didn't speak. Jewel walked in a few minutes later, glaring at her. As if transported back in time, Rowan knew the look as well as her own.

"We need to talk," Jewel announced when she sat down.

"Jewel, as I have told you on numerous occasions, your sex life needs to remain private."

Her face blanched, "I'm not talking about my sex life!"

"Oh, well that's new," she told her smiling. "But really, you should at least talk to Colt about it, don't you think? I mean. I kinda think the poor guy should know, don't you? Seems only fair, right?"

Jewel looked like she was going to combust on the spot but didn't say anything.

"Ladies!" Jolly said as he sat down. "We need to discuss something with you, Rowena."

Her eyes lifted in surprise. Jolly almost sounded unsure of himself.

"We are starting the training season and the teachers aren't releasing the children. They say it's too much for the kids and we need you to talk to them," Jewel spat out in a bored monotone.

Rowan sat up straighter. They were asking for her help? "What kind of training?"

"The usual. I want to start running them through the maze at eight. Right now, thanks to you, we have to wait until they're twelve to start weapons training. But they're too soft and I want to get to them early," Jewel answered, sounding a little more engaged.

"You want me to convince the teachers to let you start training their eight year olds?" she blurted out without thinking.

"Yes, I do. That's why you're here. To lead. So lead," Jewel snarled at her.

Rowan turned to Jolly. "I'd like to talk to you about the state of the Instructary. And I'd like to find out what the new schedule is. No one has dinners around here. No morning meetings — nothing."

Jolly smiled and sat back, nodding his head, indicating for her to continue.

"I need to look at the budgets and find money for maintenance on the buildings down there. They are falling apart around the kids."

Jewel coughed.

"Problem, Jewel?" Rowan spat at her.

"Nope. No problem at all," her voice saccharine.

"Good. When can I see the budgets?"

"When can we start training?"

Rowan sat back, thinking. It wouldn't be a bad idea

to see another drill. The intruder drill basically was watching most of the troops hide and a few people come out and take down the intruder. Not the usual fare.

"Let's do a Saturday Exercise. Without the kids first, then we can talk."

"It's Tuesday." Jewel was getting tired of this game, but Rowan was loving watching her rein in her temper.

"Are you telling me you don't want to play God? Make it Saturday! Figure it out." Rowan got up, trying to hide her smile, and walked away. They'd wanted her back; now she was, they'd just have to get used to it.

CHAPTER NINE

"Shane! Get up." Fern pounded on his door before dawn.

"Yeah," he shouted from his bed just before springing up and opening the door slightly. "What's up?"

"Saturday Exercise today. We need to get you outfitted. Get dressed."

Shane was pretty sure it was Wednesday, but nodded his head anyway and closed the door so he could throw on his clothes. He remembered Rowan talking about Saturday Exercise. *Coffee, he needed strong coffee.* After pulling on his jeans and a shirt, he stumbled out to the kitchen to make a quick cup. He was surprised to find the common area buzzing with people.

Fern found him and handed him a mug. *Oh, thank Fuck.*

"What the hell is going on?" he asked after taking a sip.

"Today has been declared Saturday. So we get to play. Rumor has it Rowena wants to assess our skills, so we're told to really impress her."

That didn't sound like the Rowan he knew, but he

nodded and gulped down more coffee. Before he knew it, they were walking down toward the Arena. The sun was just peeking over the horizon and he could see lights on in the Arena as well as the building where he knew Rowan slept. He wondered if she was sleeping now or already awake, getting ready.

Fern hustled him into the basement where there were piles of Teflon vests, weapons, and ammo. *Jesus, this place's a stockpile of every weapon imaginable.* Shane whistled in appreciation.

"Yeah, it's cool down here. Have you ever used a gun before? Like a real one—not a video game one?"

"Um, yeah, once or twice." Shane swallowed a smile.

Fern nodded and went to work searching through the piles. Soon Shane had his own vest, a side arm, and a rifle, as well as enough ammo to win a battle. And sunglasses. He did note that he wasn't offered ear protection or proper eye protection. The two dollar sunglasses were probably going to be more of a hindrance than actual protection, but he took them and followed Fern back outside.

He stood around and listened to the chatter while Fern geared up. Soon everyone looked ready and he could feel the excitement in the air. Fern indicated he should look up; when he did he saw a deck with large windows surrounding it.

"That's where they are right now, watching us. Make no mistake, they see everything. If you fuck up, they'll see it."

"The Deck House?"

"Yup. The Deck House. Jewel is up there right now thinking up horrendous things for us to do. No one gets out without some catastrophe. And everyone that's not down here with us is in there, waiting to mess with you and fuck you up. Stay awake, my friend."

Shane watched him as he spoke, Fern's eyes getting larger and larger, looking more freaked out by the second. What the hell was going down?

"In the Deck House?"

"No. In the maze." Fern motioned his head toward the back of where they were standing.

Shane had never heard of the maze, but he turned to see what Fern was talking about. There was a large structure behind them. *Well, this just gets better and better, doesn't it?*

"Hellloo Lovers!" Jolly's voice boomed over the loud speakers sitting on the Deck House. "Today we have a special treat for you. Here is your training officer, the lovely Jewel, to explain it all to you. And as always, Disarm and Protect!"

"Disarm and Protect!" The crowd shouted back, taking Shane by surprise. The night of the break in came flooding back to him with Justin screaming that exact phrase to Rowan through the window.

"Troops!" Jewel's voice boomed over the speakers, "Here are the rules: get through the maze. Don't kill anyone. If you run into an injured party, you must administer first aid. You can work together but it's every person for themself in there. You cannot move forward without achieving all your targets, Rio." She paused long enough for the crowd to chuckle. "And watch out for the sirens. Boys, don't let your little head do all the thinking in there!"

A whoop flew in the air and she signed off. People started making their way toward the maze and Shane could see a long line forming. This was going to take forever. Fern hadn't left his side; he supposed he was on new-guy duty. Shane checked his gun and dry fired a few rounds while he waited in the line.

"You look like you know what you're doing there. Anything you want to tell me?" Fern asked him.

"Nope. Like I said, I've handled a gun a few times before. This sounds serious, so I thought I'd get acquainted."

Just then shots rang out in the air, four in a row, three, five, then nothing. He heard shouts, but couldn't hear what they were saying. Soon more shots, but there were too many to gauge what they were shooting at.

He noticed a nervous looking boy ahead of him. He was geared out and standing next to a tall, older gentleman talking to him. "I'll have your shoulder the whole time. You just worry about shooting and I'll guide you. I'm just your guide, you do the rest," he heard the man say to the boy.

Jesus, that kid looked like he was barely twelve. Justin said he started weapons training at five. Back then, that's how they did it. Thanks to Rowan, now they had to wait until the kids were twelve. Justin told him he had nightmares for years after he started doing the Saturday Exercises.

Gun shots filled the air, making it harder to hear around him. They were getting closer and closer to the front. He watched as the boy and his guide stepped up to the mark. A young man with a clipboard and a watch nodded at them. The guide grabbed the boy's shoulder and pushed him into the maze. They disappeared from view, but he could hear them screaming commands at each other.

"Dude, you're not my guide, are you?" Shane asked Fern as they stepped up together.

"Yeah, but don't worry, I only haul your ass around

if you clam up in there." Fern smiled, his big teeth showing.

Shane nodded and stepped up to the mark.

"Ready?" clipboard guy asked.

"Always," Shane answered.

Clipboard guy looked up and smiled, "I like this one. He's cocky as hell. Don't worry, you won't want to puke till mid-way."

Before Shane could ask about that he got the nod and Fern shoved him into the maze. At the first turn there were four large barrels with paper targets attached to them, each one representing what Shane could barely make out as different presidents. Shane took out his weapon, aimed and fired. The shot went wildly off to the right. *What the hell?* His weapon wasn't calibrated at all.

He compensated and hit his mark. Four targets made and he ran to the next corner, where he found three more, this time flying high in the wind. After easily shooting close to the bullseye in each one, he turned and found five more. That was what he expected, after this he was flying blind.

The maze wasn't that tall, just enough to make it hard to tell what's coming. The pathway was dusty, layered with innumerable footprints. Fern was right behind him the entire time. As he trotted around the next corner scanning for hazards or traps, he heard a cry for help. He looked at Fern who shrugged. He got it, Fern was just there to haul his ass out if he froze, until then he was just following.

The maze had tightened with corners almost on top of each other. They rounded another corner and heard it again. "Help! Please, help me." Shane listened closely and recognized the voice as Star. What was it that Jewel said, don't think with your little head? Star was a trap. He came around another corner and there she was, covered in blood, lying on the ground. He ran without thinking with either head.

"Jesus, Star. Where are you hurt?" He ran his hands up and down her body looking for injury. He knew that this was just an exercise so it had to be fake blood, but god, it smelled real.

"Shane. I knew you'd come. They said you'd leave me here." She yelped when he ran his hand over her shoulder. He could feel it was out of place.

"They dislocated your shoulder for a fucking exercise? What the fuck?" He turned to Fern for help. "Get your ass over here. Hold her down while I put her shoulder back in."

Star's eyes widened and she started to speak, but nothing came out of her mouth. She was on some pretty heavy drugs right now, that was for sure. Knowing she was really hurt, he wanted to find the source of all this blood. These people were animals to make her suffer like this.

"Okay, this is going to hurt a little. Fern, get behind her and hold her hips, I'm going to pop this shoulder back in, the pain should stop once it gets back in."

He waited for Fern to get in position before grabbing her wrist and bracing his foot just under her shoulder. "On three. One, two, three." He pulled and let the shoulder slip back in its place. Star passed out immediately, falling limply on Fern. "What the fuck is wrong with you people?"

Fern slid out from under her and stood. "Come on man, let's go. That took way too much time."

"She's covered in blood! What else did they do to her?"

"Nothing man, that's sheep's blood. Let's move."

Shane hesitated for a second, but with no other

option, he nodded and followed Fern around the next corner.

• • •

Rowan watched from her place inside the Deck House as Shane and Fern discussed something over Star's unconscious body. She wished she could hear what they were saying, but at this point she was almost numb with shock herself. She knew Shane was going to stop and help her. All the others walked right on by, but there was no way Shane would walk away from an injured person. She shuddered about what he would do when he found the animals.

She knew Jewel was intense, crazy even, but this— this was beyond her worst nightmares. They'd always used a few people to pretend to be hurt, or set some traps to confuse the troops, but what Jewel had set up was sickening. And she was exposing it all to Shane, the kindest soul she knew. This was her fault, all of it. Everything that was happening to him was because of her.

The maze was full now and it was hard to keep track of everything that was going on, but with Shane and Fern being the only people to stop and help Star, the entire Deck House watched the scene unfold before them. Jewel had put her there as a distraction, to see who would waste time helping her. Everyone else knew that and had kept going.

"Well, well, looks like that new recruit knows how to handle a gun and how to do field medicine, even if he is a little soft," Jewel was saying to Jolly.

Rowan's hair stood on end. The last thing she wanted was to have Jewel take an interest in Shane. Screaming from the maze brought her attention back down to the drama. She watched as Shane fought off his attacker. At first he was holding back, but when Rio punched him hard in the gut, she could see Shane's entire body shift to full fight. His movements got faster and his punches got harder. Finally, he landed one square in the face and Rio went down like a ton of bricks.

Out, yes, but for how long? She remembered vividly when she'd fought off her attacker and thought she had knocked him out, only to discover him awake and on top of her before she even got her bearings back. The bruises had taken weeks to heal—he claimed he only wanted her to learn to never let her guard down—ever.

Fern and Shane rounded the corridor with the animals. All of them near death now, having been bleeding for hours. Shane fell to his knees at the first one while his hands ran over its body. He paused and looked up at the Deck House, his disdain clear from here. Pulling out his weapon while shaking his head, he fired one round straight into the animal's head.

Rowan choked on her tears, her heart breaking, no longer able to put up a brave face about the whole thing. She had started to freak out when they first brought the sheep out there, but was shut down by Jolly. Now she sat with the entire crew and watched as he slowly walked up to each and every animal and did the same. He first checked to see how far gone they were, aimed, and fired. As he stood over the last animal, he fired and fell to his knees, roaring in agony. Tears ran unabashed down her face, his anguish too much to stop them. She was sure he had never witnessed such cruelty, while it seemed as if everyone else here was almost immune to it.

"Just fascinating!" Jolly said while watching.

"Yeah, except now everyone behind him can't practice their field dressings," Jewel said, sounding irritated.

"Look, we've pushed him to the breaking point. He got pretty far for a first timer, he'll thank us for jolting his system when he settles," Jolly said, thoroughly enjoying himself and pointing to Fern and Shane.

Shane was walking away from his targets, refusing to participate, and Fern was arguing with him. Shane tried handing over his gun, but Fern refused to take it. Rowan bit back more tears while her stomach churned. She had to physically stop herself from walking right out the door and running straight to him. He needed her, she could see that from here; he was here for her and look at him. She knew it would take years to recover from this.

She watched him walk out of the maze and disappear in the crowd of people. Try as she might, she could not let her eyes focus on the rest of the maze. There was nothing left she needed to see. If this was how things had evolved here over the last few years, there was no way the eight year olds were starting weapons training, hell, if she had her way, she'd move that age up again. And she'd ban the use of animals.

"So, what do you think, Your Majesty. Impressive, aren't they?" Jewel turned to her as the last of the troops made their way through the maze.

"Impressive might not be the word, Jewel. Horrific is more like it. But I'll reserve judgment until I see the times. We can meet after that." Rowan stood and walked out, listening to Jewel seethe behind her.

~

Breath, Run, Breath, Run. Rowan made her way as

quickly as possible down the path. She needed something familiar, something to ground her. Her mind kept replaying Shane shooting every single animal, putting them out of their misery. By the time she got to the Instructary, tears poured over her face once again, clouding her vision.

"Rowena!" Cheri called behind her.

Of course she was close behind. God forbid Rowan take two steps without a babysitter. What the hell was she going to do, run away in broad daylight? *Maybe.*

"Cheri, please. I just need a moment. I'm going home."

Cheri ran to catch up as Rowan stopped to talk to her.

"It's only going to get worse. I've seen her plans. I honestly think she has lost her mind." Cheri paused to catch her breath, "She's going to kill us all. You are the only one who can stop this madness. I know it's hard, but Jolly listens to you. Or at least, he will listen. If you're going to stay, you need to know. It's only gonna get worse."

Rowan watched as Cheri turned and headed back up the path, leaving her alone. Did Cheri just confide in her? If she was going to stay? As if that was still a question? How could the training get worse? They were already slaughtering animals in the name of practicing field dressings. They were already using people as traps and distractions. How much worse could it get?

She couldn't take the thought and heaved unexpectedly. Leaning over she threw up the entire contents of her stomach and then some. Once again, tears streamed down her face and sobs wracked her body when the dry heaving allowed her to cry. This place needed to go up in flames.

"Rowan?" Lina's hand was on her back, wrapping around her waist and pulling her into a hug. "I know, sweetie. I know."

"What the hell has been going on here? This place is toxic," Rowan almost yelled at her.

Lina dragged her inside, leading her to her old room. Rowan was hardly aware of her surroundings as she sat on the bed. Soon a cold cloth was on her face and Lina was handing her a glass of water.

"Lina. She used Star out there. And so many animals. And they weren't just hurt, they were all dying. They were all bleeding to death and he just shot them. All of them, one by one. I saw him. He just lost it. What have I done?" She broke down in tears again thinking about Shane and the memories he would have to live with the rest of his life.

"It's been like this for a while now. We're doing what we can to keep the kids out of it, but the adults talk, so they know what's happening. Jewel just keeps getting more and more harsh," Lina started when Rowan had calmed down, "I heard about the new recruit. If you can stop this, Ro. Please. I don't know how serious you are about staying, but please, if you can you've got to stop Jewel."

"Why didn't you tell me?"

Lina laughed, "Tell you what? That Jewel has lost her mind? That you should come back because it's so bad here? What would that have accomplished? You didn't need to know."

"Lina. Are they feeding you guys down here? You mentioned before that they were using food as an incentive, but now, after seeing that—Jesus. Are they starving the kids?"

Lina smiled sadly and looked up at the ceiling. "That's over now. We kept the kids well fed, but they said we were over budget, so they cut back on meals. It was the traveling. But things are better now."

Rowan looked at her friend and the weight of her words poured down on her. Lina traveled to find her in spite of the punishment, and Rowan couldn't get her act together to see her, prolonging the agony here. Right then, she vowed to do everything in her power to fix that. She would use her influence to protect them. All of them; the kids, the animals, Lina, the rest of the troops. Might she have the power to stop the suffering? If she agreed to everything Jolly wanted from her, could she influence the way things were done around here? If so, it was time she started.

CHAPTER TEN

Throwing the gear on the floor the moment he walked into his room, Shane stripped and jumped in the shower. *What. The. Fuck.* These people were beyond anything he could have ever imagined. He expected a bunch of overzealous devotees spouting the virtues of their lifestyle. He was prepared for martial arts and weapons training. Hell, he even expected people to jump out at him in that fucking maze.

Never in his life did he ever think they would brutalize animals and leave them scattered in the maze to slowly bleed to death. And what the fuck did they do to Star? Drug her and pull her shoulder out? How many times did they do that to her, how many people before him put her shoulder back in? Why would she allow that to happen to her?

The thought made him want to puke. He turned the water hotter and let it soak into his skin. He needed to get Rowan the fuck out. Now. There was no point in hanging around. They had to leave tonight. He couldn't take much more of this. His life was waiting for him and he needed to get back to it.

Too quickly, the water ran cold and he stepped out of the shower stall. It sounded as if there were people in his room. He must have left the radio on. Drying off, he walked into his room to find Eden and another woman in his room. Grabbing his towel, he flung it around his waist.

"Can I help you, ladies?" he spit out, none too happy.

The strange woman watched him carefully, "I don't think we've had the pleasure of meeting yet. I'm Storm." She held out her hand for him to shake.

He made a big show of switching hands to hold his towel and then slowly shaking her hand.

"Nice to meet you. Now's not the best time. Do you mind if I get dressed?"

Storm's eyes flashed at his request, "Of course, Shane. I just wanted to come in and check on you. You seemed out of sorts after today's exercise."

Shane snorted, "You could say that."

"Shane," Eden said, "If you need anything, just ask, okay?"

There was something about her voice, her eyes, he couldn't place it, but he got cold shivers every time she spoke to him, and he avoided her at all costs.

"How's Star?" he asked, leveling his eyes at Storm.

He knew she was a leader right alongside of Jolly, and it seemed as if she acquiesced to Jolly on a lot of things, pedophilia, child rape, abuse, assault and battery, kidnapping, to name a few. He had to wonder if she approved of this morning's exercise.

"Star is fine. I'm sure you'll see her at dinner," Storm answered, matching his tone.

With that the two women turned and left him alone. *Dinner, yeah right.* Like he was going to sit and break bread with these people. No fucking way. He was waiting in this room until they all went to bed, then he and Rowan were getting the fuck out of Dodge.

Now he wished he had brought a phone. Justin had been convinced he'd be searched and they'd take it, but so far no one had even asked to see his backpack. It'd be nice to chill out and read the news while he waited. He checked the time. It was after four, too many hours until he could flee. He flopped on his bed and closed his eyes, knowing they were almost free of this dreaded place.

~

Shane awoke with a start, the dinner bell fading away. Sitting up, he shook his head, trying to clear the dense fog that seemed to have settled over him while he slept. Quietly, he put his ear to the door, listening for sounds outside. He could hear the kitchen crew clanging dishes together, doors opening as people started filing in, and the dreaded 'natural voice' these maniacs performed nightly.

Checking the lock, he confirmed his door was still secure before starting to pack. He wanted to be ready to jump when the time was right. With only a handful of things to throw into his pack, he was ready within minutes. Now, nothing left to do but wait.

He was used to waiting. Made him think about all those stakeouts with Cody and Rob, something, he thought ironically, he missed. Who would have thought he'd miss a stakeout. Truth be told, he missed his life. Setting aside the horrific events of the day, he just didn't understand the appeal of living in a large group like this. There was no privacy, no choice, no spontaneity. The routine was set in stone and never wavered.

And the people! Shane just didn't understand why anyone would want to live with all these people. The dramas these people went through on an hourly basis. The bickering was never ending. Almost as if they were compensating for handing over their souls upon arrival, everyone held on to the most ridiculous and trivial things. He had witnessed a full house meeting to discuss what type of milk to buy, 2% or fat free. Good God! The level of discontent was off the charts. Not since high school had Shane experienced so much ill will among peers. Over milk, no less. But everyone appeared to be okay with assault, kidnapping, and animal cruelty. Rowan was right, there was no explaining it—this place was ass backwards.

A soft knock on the door startled him out of his thoughts.

"Shane?" Star quietly called through the door.

Without thinking, Shane jumped at the sound of her voice and opened the door.

"Are you okay?" he asked.

"Why aren't you at dinner?" she whispered.

"Star, why are you out of bed? Your shoulder should be really sore. Where's your sling?"

"Shhh. Come one. Let's go to dinner," she whispered again.

He stepped back and shook his head. There was no way he could eat with those people. Every single one of them went through that maze; his stomach would revolt.

"Shane, you have to come to dinner."

"No, actually I don't. Where's your sling?" he spoke with his voice at full volume.

Star paled at his loud voice. She looked desperate, "Please whisper."

Taking a deep breath, he pulled his head out of ass. These people took their dinner rituals as serious as Catholics took communion and he was being offensive.

He needed to maintain as much cover as he could tonight to ensure their escape.

"I'm sorry," he whispered, "I just can't come to dinner. I just. I don't feel well." He felt like an ass wimping out and lying, but he thought that would be the least offensive thing he could say.

"Is it your stomach? You can stay in your room if you feel like you might have the stomach flu." She seemed to be prompting him.

Frustrated that she still hadn't answered his question about her sling, he bit back another question about it and simply nodded his head.

"Okay. You stay here then. I'll come check on you after dinner."

Shane watched her turn and walk out, silently closing the door behind her. Un-fucking-believable. Just this morning, someone dislocated her shoulder and drugged her, yet here she was convincing him to break bread with the same people that assaulted her.

Lying back down on the bed, he listened to the sounds of dinner. He heard the play and sounds of dessert plates being passed out. Wondering if now would be a good time to sneak off, he decided against it. Rowan would be having her own dinner right about now with the likes of Jolly, Jewel, and the rest of their inner circle.

He would wait. Let them think he was sick. They'd leave him alone and he would steal away in the night.

• • •

When the kitchen noises finally quieted down, he got up and listened at his door again. Nothing. The Big House was finally quiet. He grabbed his backpack and opened the door. His heart leapt into his throat when Star's sleeping body fell into his room.

"What the hell?"

"Oh, hey," Star's sleepy voice croaked from the floor.

"What in God's name are you doing?" Shane asked, trying to hide his pack.

"I was worried about you. So I was checking on you."

"By sleeping on my door?"

"Well, I was just—just making sure you were okay. I didn't hear anything, so I figured you were asleep."

Shane didn't buy her story for a minute. *Checking on me, my ass.* She was guarding his door.

"Star. You need to go to bed. This is ridiculous. You're hurt and need sleep to heal." He started to haul her up.

"Can I just stay with you? That way if you get sick in the night, I can help you." She slurred her words, obviously exhausted, and held her shoulder as if still in pain.

"No sweetheart, you can't stay here. You need to go to bed. You need help getting there?"

Star finally looked at him and shook her head once. "No, I can get there. I'll come check on you in the morning, then. Night, Shane," she said, reaching up to kiss him.

Moving his head to ensure her kiss landed on his check, he smiled tightly and led her out of his room. Standing in the hallway, he watched her walk down the hall and disappear into a room. He turned, thankful that ended swiftly, only to run smack into Storm.

"Looks like you're feeling better," Storm said, walking right up to his room.

"Um, yes. Thank you."

"Was that Star I just saw leaving?"

Shane's eyes narrowed, "Yup. Funny enough, I just found her sleeping on my door. That girl should be in bed, on meds, and her arm should be in a sling. Is there a sling on the property? Or I don't know, maybe someone should have taken her to a hospital."

Her entire body language changed. She stood up taller, her shoulders pushed out and down, her leg muscles grew taut, and her eyes widened and became brighter. Shane recognized the signs; she was gearing up for a fight.

"Star knows her own limits. Something I think you need to work on. How are you adjusting these days? I sense you're having a hard time settling."

"Settling? I was settling just fine until this morning."

"So this morning's exercise created unease. What part of your past do you think is causing such uneasiness?"

Is she fucking serious? Shane had to remember to close his mouth. His past made him uneasy about this morning?

"I'm sorry, I'm not following you?"

Storm smiled at him as if he was a poor, stupid boy. "Often people come here to let go of their old lives and start anew. You're obviously stuck. Holding on to something out there that is preventing you from fully embracing this opportunity that has been presented to you. This morning seemed to really shake you up." She paused and tilted her head as if waiting for his inner self to burst forward, "You should meditate on that and see what breaks loose. Often right before a major breakthrough, the body will resist and get sick. I'd say you're about to enter a new level."

He didn't know what to say so he just nodded his

head and left her in the hall. Locking the door he stared at it, waiting for something to happen. Not having a clue what she was talking about, he wasn't really sure how to proceed. A major breakthrough? New level? New level of what? Madness, complete insanity.

Walking around his room, he felt as if the walls were closing in on him. He listened at the door and heard people in the hall. He needed to get the hell out of here. He decided to try the window. Rushing to the window and throwing open the curtains, he discovered the window was painted shut. *Damn it.*

He needed a new plan. There was no way they were going to leave him alone tonight, that much he had figured out, but how the hell was he going to get to Rowan and get the hell off this property? He could walk right out the front door and no one would fight too hard to stop him, at least he hoped that was still true, but Rowan was a different story entirely.

Sliding his backpack under his bed, he sat and thought. Sooner or later he'd come up with a plan and then they'd leave together.

CHAPTER ELEVEN

"Why don't we have dinners together?" Rowan asked the group.

Jolly, Storm, Jewel, and a few others including Colt were all gathered in the common room having breakfast together. These were the people that had segregated themselves from the rest of the community and she wanted to know why.

"And speaking of dinners, what happened to morning meetings? Since when do we separate so much. This entire group has splintered off."

"Since it became clear that people like us have no business wasting our precious energy dealing with them," Jewel almost growled at her.

"Wasting your precious energy? Like what, you're so enlightened you just can't be bothered with the little people?" Rowan shot back at her, "Storm, is this something you agree with?"

She knew she was putting her on the spot, but Jewel's constant attitude was proof of just how broken this community was.

Storm cleared her throat before speaking, "I think there is some merit to her argument. We all agreed as separate as our tasks are these days, two separate meetings made sense. And dinners just sort of evolved that way."

"You people are all asleep. Basking in your own self-importance. Talk about group animal. All of you." She glared at Jolly and Jewel, "You have isolated yourselves and no one can call you out on your own shit."

The slow clapping startled her. Jolly stood slowly, clapping his hands: Clap. Clap. Clap.

"Rowena. I'm so proud of you. You are finally able to see how much you hate change. You were always so attached to things and here you are back not a few days and already trying to get things as you remember them."

She froze. The ice in Jolly's eyes told her she had gone too far. *So much for helping these people.* The only question now was how far Jolly would go in his reprimand.

"I think she has a point," Storm said, surprising everyone in the room, "Oh come on Jolly, she's not that off. A lot has changed since Rowena left us."

Jolly's head whipped around to face Storm. Rowan watched, speechless. Storm had never come to her defense before. No matter how much she agreed with you, Storm believed you needed to fight your own battles, even if fighting left you bloodied and bruised on the floor.

"I, for one, have too many other things to do to talk about Rowena. I'll be in my office actually working." Jewel stood as she spoke, effectively breaking the tension in the room.

Jolly and Storm seemed to have had a silent conversation and he too turned and left the room. Slowly, the others got up one by one and meandered out of the room. Soon there was just Rowan and Storm left.

"Rowena, I need your help," Storm said when they were alone.

Her head snapped up, "Uh, okay."

"There's a new recruit on site who is right on the cusp of a breakthrough, but seems to be resisting. Star has tried her best, but they just aren't connecting. I was wondering if you would like to speak to him."

"Yeah," she blurted out before thinking, "I mean, yes, if you think it will help."

"I do. His name is Shane. I'll send him up here this morning. I think the library will be a pleasant meeting place, don't you?"

Rowan nodded her head, afraid to speak. Cheri had taken her to the new library earlier and it was a beautiful space, full to the brim with books. Of course, each book had been hand selected by Jolly to make sure the troops were reading the right things. Most of the books were things he had written over the years. But still, the space felt heavenly.

She couldn't believe that Storm wanted her to talk to Shane. Apparently her outburst this morning did accomplish one thing: it proved to everyone that her commitment to stay was real. Real enough to start talking to the new recruits.

She was almost too nervous to move, but she stood and walked to the library. The morning had not gone as planned at all. She had wanted to start a conversation about the craziness in the community. Jewel's thirst for blood, the training, the lack of funds for the kids, withholding food, and separate dinners. The community was splintering, hard. People were scared.

Pacing the room, she tried to think of what to say to Shane. Did she pretend they had never met? Was someone watching them? There was always someone watching. She would need to find a private place to talk to him.

A throat cleared behind her. Rowan turned to find Fern and Shane standing in the doorway.

"Hello Rowena. This is Shane. Storm said you wanted to talk to him," Fern said, head down, not looking at her.

Rowan forced her eyes off Shane and looked at Fern, "Thank you, Fern. It's nice to see you again."

Fern looked up and smiled at her. "It's nice to see you again, Ro."

Neither Shane nor Rowan spoke while Fern left the room. Rowan walked over to the door and shut it before forcing her voice to work. "Please, have a seat, Shane."

He moved to a large chair and sank into it. Rowan studied him and did not like what she saw. His eyes were bloodshot and he looked exhausted. His hair looked dirty and his skin seemed to have lost its healthy glow. Just then, the door slowly opened. She waited, but no one entered the room.

"How long have you been traveling?" Rowan asked him pleasantly.

Shane's eyes narrowed and he was about to speak, but Rowan held up her finger and gave him a warning look. She hoped like hell he understood, people were watching, listening.

"About six months," Shane told her.

"And what inspired you to hit the road?"

Shane's slow smile told her a lot more than anything he could have said, "I'm seeking. Life just felt empty and alone—like something crucial was missing. I needed to find it. Wherever it was."

Her insides melted as she listened to his deep, velvety voice. His eyes flashed, giving her a knowing look that warmed her heart.

"I see. We are all seeking something. Tell me about your stay here. How do you like it?" Rowan was running down the list of questions they were supposed to ask in these small interventions, thankful to have a script to guide her.

"My stay here. Well, it's been enlightening. I think I could have skipped yesterday all together. Don't you?" His eyes became dark, almost black, as he spoke about yesterday.

"I take it you didn't enjoy Saturday Exercise?"

He stopped moving and just looked at her. The sadness that showed in his face made her want to cry. He put his head down, "I can't do this, Rowan," he whispered, "Please."

Reaching out, she grabbed his leg, soaking up his body heat. He leaned his head on her hand and sighed. Not knowing what to do, she leaned down and kissed the back of his head.

"I'm so sorry," she whispered.

They sat like that for a moment before she remembered where they were. Springing off the chair, she knew it was time to leave. "Let's go outside, shall we?"

He stood and followed her out. They wound their way through the building and finally found the exterior door. The blinding sun streamed into the hallway as she opened the door, waiting for Shane to follow her. Silent still, they walked quite a ways from the building before Rowan dared to open her mouth.

"Shane, you need to leave. This place will eat you up and spit you out."

"And what will it do to you?" he snapped back quickly.

She smiled and looked at the sky, trying to look as if they were having a pleasant conversation. She didn't know where, but someone was watching them.

"I saw what happened yesterday. I don't want you to go through that again. Please, Shane. Go home."

"How in the hell can you tell me that?" He whipped his head around, grabbing her arm, stopping their movement.

Carefully and oh so gracefully, she placed one hand on top of his and looked up, "They are watching us," before looking directly at him, "I have work to do here. These people need me."

• • •

Shane couldn't believe his ears, didn't trust his brain. "Have you lost your mind? What are they holding over your head? Why are you fighting me on this? It's me. Rowan, come on."

"Shane, you have a life outside. I can tell you're still attached to it. You're just not ready to let go of what you've left behind. My advice to you would be to go home and see if you can make your life happy there. I just don't see you working out here long term. You just don't have what it takes." Rowan spoke to him as if he was a stranger and that infuriated him.

Her eyes flashed again and he remembered her warning. People were everywhere. He nodded and squeezed her arm gently, "I don't think I'm quite ready to give up just yet," he spoke, barely able to contain the fury he felt.

She dropped his hand and they continued their walk.

"So tell me, Rowena, what are your plans, now that you're back."

If she was taken aback by his question, she didn't show it. Shane did notice that her movements continued to be graceful and her eyes continued to scan the area around them.

"There have been a lot of changes since I have been away and I hope to get us back on course. The Instructary needs repairs and the children need more food."

"Food?"

"Yes, I guess they are low on funds so their food stores are low. And I'd like to review the training procedures."

"Training procedures. Is that what you all call it?"

"You all? Careful Shane, your true colors are showing through. Like I said, I just don't think you have what it takes to survive a place like this. You need to be ruthless and self-centered. And above all, you need to include yourself. You still see yourself as separate."

Shane tripped on a rock in the path. What was she telling him? Why was she including herself with these people? He needed to just talk to her, alone.

"Is there a place we can go?" he asked, looking up at the sky.

After a moment or two, she nodded and led them toward the Instructary. Without speaking they followed the path that led down the hill to a large building. At the moment it was quiet, but he had heard the kids playing nearby moments before.

Rowan slipped into a small building with Shane close behind her. She walked down a hall and out the other side. He waited while she pulled the door open to a shed. Stepping inside, he saw tricycles, sand toys, and other outside equipment stacked neatly in piles. She pulled the door closed and turned to face him.

All of his resistance fell away the moment he knew they were finally alone. He wrapped his arms around her and held on for life. At first he felt her try to push away, but within seconds she fell into his body. Before

Shane could even say anything, her hands were in his hair and shivers were racing up and down his body.

"Baby. I love you. Oh God, I missed you," he said.

"I love you, Shane. I'm so sorry."

He hovered over her, his lips so close to hers, yet he waited. His heart soared at her admission. Just as he was about to slam down on her mouth, her soft lips reached up and caressed his tenderly, making his heart melt on the spot.

Slowly at first, he kissed her, but the heat took over and soon his kiss was hot enough to melt steel. When she opened her mouth, inviting him in, his cock sprang to life. While rubbing against her, he drank from her as a dying man would at a well in the desert. Moaning deeply, she held his hair and wrapped her legs around him. His fingertips found the skin just under her shirt, scorching him as he sought out more.

Suddenly she pulled back, her chest heaving with the effort.

"No," she growled, "You need to leave." Her voice was so low and thick, Shane barely recognized it.

"Not without you," he growled back.

He watched her, challenging her to run from him, kiss him again, anything. She paced between the tricycles and the four square balls while her breathing slowed.

"This is not okay. I need to stay here. You need to go. You don't understand, I can't leave now. It's too late."

"What are you talking about, Rowan? Too late for what? Justin is waiting for you. Your son."

"I know he's my son. That is all I know."

"What, then? Make me understand."

"There's nothing to understand. If you don't leave, I'll tell them you're a PI looking for someone." Her eyes were cold when she spoke to him. Shane was taken aback with her tone and her threat.

He took a slow, deep breath, waiting for her to calm down. "What have they done to you? What did he do to you?"

He stormed over to her and thrust her body into the light, scanning her neck, her arms, lifting her shirt to check her back and stomach. He wanted to see her legs but with her jeans on he knew that wasn't going to happen.

"Stop it!" She pushed him away. "Nothing. I don't have any marks on me."

"Just on your soul. Mark my words Rowan, they have damaged you. This is not over."

He stormed out the door, not able to handle another second. How could she stand there and tell him she had to stay, that he didn't understand, that he needed to leave—to threaten him? Running back up the path to the Big House, he brushed the tears out of his eyes. She had kissed him. She had held him and he'd thought—just for a second, he thought she was back.

He knew he had waited too long. She was left here in the hands of these animals for far longer than he ever meant. They had damaged her, he could see the scars in her eyes. He didn't know what exactly they did, but he vowed revenge. No longer did he have a singular goal here. By the time he reached the Big House, he was bound and determined to destroy this place and Jolly right along with it.

CHAPTER TWELVE

"Hey Shane, we're over here," Fern shouted as he approached the crew. They were still tearing apart the old barn. The usual suspects were scattered around doing various tasks.

"Where you been?" Beck asked, only slightly accusatory.

"Had to go meet with Rowena."

That gave everyone pause. The work stopped around them as the men gathered to hear.

"Really? You?" Beck asked him.

"Yup." Shane nodded his head, not offering any more information than necessary.

"So, is it true?" Fern asked.

"Is what true?"

"That she's fucking nuts. That living on the streets did her in. That Jolly sent her out there and it destroyed her?" Fern explained.

Shane's first reaction was to defend her, but stopped himself, "You could say that, yeah," he told him slowly, a plan forming in his head.

Beck started laughing and a few of the other men whistled.

"I knew it. She just looked fucked up when Jolly

made that big announcement. I think she lost her shit out there. That's the problem with these lifers, they just can't handle it anywhere but here," Beck said.

"She looked alright to me this morning when I dropped you off," Fern disagreed.

Shane laughed, "Well, you should have stuck around. Man, she's not playing with a full deck of cards. I know you all hope she's going to be the one to take you to the next level and all that—just saying."

The other men nodded and went back to work. Shane picked up his shovel and started moving dirt with Fern and Beck, ignoring the raw churning in his stomach. Could he really do this to her? Damn straight, if destroying Rowan's credibility helped break their hold over her, he was all in. For the first time in months he felt like he was back in control. If the people rejected her as a leader, there was no reason for her to be here, was there?

• • •

Jolly looked over at her like a father doting proudly on his daughter. Fighting the urge to kick him, Rowan kept speaking to the overly crowded room.

"Again, we are going to try a few changes going forward. Some of them will feel like going back to the way things used to be, and some of them are just new. But again, I think, in the end, everyone will be happy."

Ugh, why can't she just complete a sentence like a normal person? She watched the looks being thrown around the room. It was pretty clear some of them thought she had lost her mind, but given her status she knew they would placate her.

"The first major change will be dinners. We have all

agreed that sitting down and eating together is very important, so starting tonight, we are all going to eat here in the Big House. It might be a little tight, but we can manage it.

"The second change will be a full morning meeting. However, we will need to start the meeting a wee bit earlier than normal, so I'm thinking we should start at 7 am."

A loud groan went around the room. She didn't understand, everyone seemed to complain that there were separate meetings and dinners and now that she was bringing them all back together, no one seemed happy about it.

"And the last one for now is a Saturday Crew to help get the building maintenance under control. Starting with the Instructary."

"What about training?" someone shouted from the back.

Rowan paused. They hadn't finished discussing training yet, Jewel had been unwilling to budge on that issue at all. She glanced at Jewel who had a smirk on her face. Rowan forced her eyes not to roll.

"We are looking into training, but given we did a Saturday Exercise midweek, we can crew this Saturday. The buildings really need it."

Having finished what she had prepared she nodded her head and sat. Slowly, people started talking among themselves. It was noon and she had gathered everyone, hoping the changes would inspire people. She had fought hard with Jolly and Jewel all morning. Storm had been absent from this morning's debate, but arrived a few minutes after Rowan starting speaking to the group.

Funny enough, Eden was there. She hardly ever showed up to these kinds of meetings. Once or twice,

Rowan had glanced her way, but her expression was unreadable. They hadn't spoken in years; long before she ran away with Justin, Eden seemed to have washed her hands of Rowan after Romano left. All those years of fighting to change things, to protect the kids, to raise the age when girls could marry, when kids had to start training, to build a school, to teach the kids to read and write, Eden never supported her. Never opposed her either, just left her completely alone.

She never understood her connection to Jolly. While Jolly was the patriarch, Storm, not Eden, was the matriarch. Eden ran the household, the food, the rooms, the people, the ins and outs of people coming and going. But she never took a more public leadership role, letting Storm take the reins. Rowan sat and wondered how her own mother could sit idly by, never offering her a hand, or support, or advice. As a mother, she could never imagine being that passive with her son. Or could she? Was she doing exactly that? No, she was fighting to protect her son every day.

People started filing out of the room. Most of the comments she overheard seemed positive, but there were a few from the men asking if she had lost her mind, or wasn't playing with a full deck, whatever that even meant.

"Rowena," Storm's icy voice brought her back to the present. "You seemed to have a positive effect on Shane yesterday. He's in much better spirits and would like to meet with you again."

She wasn't sure what to be more surprised at, Storm's arctic attitude toward her or Shane's request to see her again.

"Um, okay. I'd love to meet with him again. Would right now work?" she answered, "Storm, is everything alright?"

"That would be fine," she clipped before turning and walking out, ignoring her second question.

What on earth had gotten Storm so upset? She'd have to find out later. A quick scan of the room told her that Shane was waiting for her.

"Shall we?" Shane asked as he held the door open for her.

Rowan nodded her assent and walked with him at her heels.

"After our talk yesterday, so many things became clear, I knew that I needed to meet with you again. Thank you for taking the time from your busy schedule to see me," Shane rushed his words, almost convincing Rowan of their sincerity.

"I'm glad it helped. Another walk, perhaps? I find it so much easier to think and walk. Somehow the fresh air helps keep things in perspective." Rowan was working hard to keep the bite out of her tone.

They walked in silence, Shane leading them down the path toward the Instructary. If Rowan wasn't mistaken, Shane had a destination in mind.

"Shane, are we just walking, or are we going somewhere?"

"Aren't we always on a path to somewhere? Isn't that why we are here, so we can find our true path and arrive?"

This time Rowan let her eyes roll all the way in the back of her head. Apparently he'd been talking to his crewmates, or Star?

"Will I know when we arrive?" she asked bitterly, with thoughts of Shane and Star talking late into the night.

"Oh, the lady does not like my philosophy. I got news for ya sweetheart, around here, that is prime stuff. You say that, and people know."

"Know what?"

"Know that you're on your way to finding your path," he said breathily.

Laughing at him, she couldn't help but ask, "Who have you been talking to?"

"The guys from my barn crew. Beck, Skip, Fern. I really like Fern."

A little disgusted over how happy she was that Star was not on that list, she shook her head. Looking up, she saw the kids lining up and going inside for their afternoon classes. The playground suddenly deserted, the quiet reminded her that people could be listening.

Shane turned to her with a wolfish grin, "Come on, Ro. Perfect timing."

He grabbed her hand and started running toward the tiny school. He slipped in the door and walked briskly down the same hall before exiting into the back. She watched in awe at how quickly he seemed to own this space. Just yesterday he was a stranger here, and now he was leading her expertly back to the toy shed.

This time when she shut the door, instead of waiting for her, he was fussing with something in the back. Candle light filled the space as he spread out a blanket. There wasn't a lot of room, but just enough to make a tiny spread in the middle of the toys and bikes.

"What's all this?" How did he manage to get this down here?

"This, Ro, is for us. Come on, have a seat."

Shane settled in with his back on the ball container and she sat stiffly on the floor.

"You mean to tell me that after all those times you made me sit in those dreaded bean bags, you can't manage to get comfortable on this blanket?" he asked, smiling.

Rowan laughed in spite of herself; of course she

could get comfortable for him. She turned and backed into his lap, leaning on his chest. His body heat radiated into her skin, coaxing all the anxiety over their clandestine meeting to leak out of her.

He stroked her hair and her neck. Goosebumps erupted on her skin and she shuddered as his fingertips made their way down her arms. Leaning her head back, she closed her eyes and let the sensations wash over her.

His fingers kept up their relentless torture as they skimmed over her breasts and back up her long neck. Shane let out a shaky breath as she moaned under his ministrations. He kissed her behind her ear and bit down on her earlobe, unleashing a firestorm deep within her.

Suddenly, the memories of all the times Shane had made love to her came flooding back. Her first thought was to run, to flee from him, but the need to feel his naked body against hers, anchored her. She needed to feel his weight on top of her. Turning to face him, she crawled into his lap and kissed him. He deepened the kiss, cupping her face with his large hand.

"Shane."

"Shhh," he cut her off, "Don't talk, baby. Just feel."

He sat up and pulled her shirt off. She ran her hands through his hair, oh how she missed his silky hair. No longer spiky, but she missed running her fingers through his silk. His lips felt so soft, warm and perfect. She missed these lips and his mouth.

How could she have forgotten what being with Shane was really like? His touch scorched her skin, leaving a trail of fire and a desperate need for more. No longer worried, no longer anxious, she let her body take over—to give in, if only for a little while. She ripped his shirt off while he unclasped her bra. She felt his warm chest as her breasts brushed against him, making her nipples pebble to hard points.

Already barely breathing, she needed more. Reaching down to unbutton his jeans, she felt his hard cock throbbing under its restraint. Her eyes locked with Shane's and he smiled.

"The little guy missed you, babe."

She laughed, "Little guy? Let's not call it that. It's disingenuous. Here, stand up." She tugged on his pants.

Soon both of them were gloriously naked, Rowan wanting nothing more than to drop to her knees and take him in her mouth, but Shane stopped her. He laid back down and guided her legs over him, straddling him. She did, rubbing her core on his throbbing cock.

Growling, Shane held her hips, pushing down as she moved back and forth, getting them both slick with her desire. Rowan's brain was going to explode, she had one single desire and it wasn't this. She needed him inside her. Lifting slightly, she took him in her hand and placed him right at her entrance. She could feel him twitching in anticipation.

"You're killing me," he moaned underneath her, "Please, Rowan."

She surrounded him and slowly sunk down his cock. Feeling the stretch made her shiver. *Damn, she forgot how big he was.* Placing both hands on his hard chest, she lifted her hips, allowing her body to adjust to his width before going further. Sweat dripped off her forehead before she was fully seated. Opening her eyes, she saw the pained look on Shane's face.

"Baby?"

"Yeah?" he answered on a growl.

"Tell me what you need."

"Fuck, Rowan. I need you." He grabbed her hips

and lifted her slightly before pulling her down hard. Electricity flowed between the two of them, sparks flying as she slammed down on his hips over and over again.

Her mind snapped and she let go. No longer pretending to be Rowena, no longer a prisoner or a leader, Shane stripped all that away. Every time she slammed into his body, she felt herself rebuild. She slammed down again, harder, almost as if her soul and her orgasm were one. She desperately wanted both, tears formed as she reached her peak—her orgasm hit, exorcising Rowena and leaving the woman she had once become.

"Ahhhhh," he moaned, as he came with her, seemingly unable to control himself.

Soon, they lay together panting in the shed, listening to the quiet. She wondered if anyone heard them, how much trouble they would get into if anyone found them. What would they do to him?

"Can I ask you a question?" Shane asked before they separated.

"Yeah."

"Why? Why are you staying here?"

Her breath caught in her throat, she hesitated but was already stripped so raw, she saw no other option but the truth.

"If I stay, he leaves Justin and Talia alone. If I stay, I can protect the children and those of us that are not as bloodthirsty as Jewel. They're out of control, unstoppable. But if I stay, I can convince Jolly to stop the training. Or at least go back to what it was before Jewel took over."

"You think that's possible? To convince Jolly to do anything at all?"

"They stopped feeding the kids, Shane. Because

they had used too much of their budget. There wasn't enough food for the kids and teachers. If I'm here, I can make sure that never happens again."

Shane took a deep breath and Rowan moved off him, reaching for her clothes. She could feel Rowena creeping back in, pushing aside her stronger half. Her shoulders stooped and her stomach filled with acid. Anger lashed around, grabbing her, tying her wrists, squeezing her lungs. It was unfair—all of this was so unfair. She was Rowena now and Shane had no business reminding her of her old life. Suddenly filled with hatred she turned to him, barely able to see through the haze of red that filled her vision.

"Shane, you don't need to be here and the longer you stay the harder it'll be for you to leave. I don't have a choice. Get out now, while you still can."

CHAPTER THIRTEEN

The buzz in the Big House was non-stop. It seemed as if the only things people could talk about were Rowena and her changes to their dharma. As far as Shane could tell, no one had ever made unilateral changes like this before. Small ones, incremental steps toward a larger goal, but never one fell swoop dictated from above. People were not happy.

Shane was delighted. He roamed the halls talking to small groups, putting in his two cents about Rowena's state of mind. He learned early that he was the only one among the outer circle that had any contact with her, so his opinion carried a lot of weight. Now he just needed to find Storm.

Dinner prep was in full swing as he skirted the kitchen looking for her. The table was set plate to plate; there wasn't even enough room for all the chairs. The way he saw it, people were going to need to stand to fit everyone. All the more reason to smile—tonight was step one in Rowan's downfall as leader. He could barely contain his excitement. Their afternoon in the shed proved to him that she was still his Rowan. It had been brief, but he saw the real Rowan and wanted more of her. She had been damaged, he could see that, and she had some ass backward logic about her role in this place, but Shane knew with his whole heart that she wanted nothing to do with any of this. She just needed a little push.

"Storm, there you are. Some of the other guys had a question for you," Shane said as he approached his target.

"Hello, Shane. How are you feeling?" Storm asked him with what felt like false concern.

"Oh, great. Thanks for asking. The guys wanted to know—oh you know what, that's right, they figured out that Rowena was in charge now. I think they sent someone to find her. Sorry, my bad." He smiled at her, waiting.

Storm stared at him blankly as she fully registered what he'd just said. "Um, wait. What did they need to know?"

"I'm not sure, something about tomorrow's crew. The overall plan, timelines, something about what's on the critical path. But I think they covered all that with Rowena. I just forgot she's taking over for you. So sorry to trouble you." Shane started to walk away.

"Shane!" Storm's sharp command stopped him. He fought off the smile before turning around to face her.

"Yeah."

"Since when is Rowena in charge of crews?"

"Don't ask me, I'm just the new guy." He threw his hands in the air, trying to look as innocent as possible, "So, what are you going to do with all your free time? Are you, like, retiring now?"

He watched as Storm's face went from slightly flushed to angry red. She never spoke, but her eyes were throwing darts before she turned around and walked away. If he wasn't mistaken, he could see her trembling as she walked down the hall. Mission accomplished.

~

Walking into the dining room, Shane was taken aback with how crowded it was. The room was full of people milling about practicing their dreaded natural voice and waving their arms over their heads, swinging their hips. They looked like skinny chimpanzees in some mating ritual. Having been around a few weeks, he was no longer excused from the exercise, so he too belted out a low om and rotated his hips with the rest of them.

While waving his arms like some deranged gorilla, he scanned the room. He saw Jolly doing the same, belting out deep, loud oms of his own. He also noted several new people he hadn't seen before. Jewel stuck out like a sore thumb on a debutante's hand. Mussed curly hair that fell in jagged layers around her shoulders, full lips with high cheekbones, tight pants and a half shirt that barely covered her large breasts, swinging unrestrained from a bra. Exactly the way Rob described her.

This time it was Jolly, not Lisa, who picked up his plate and started serving himself from the buffet line. Shane grabbed his plate, still next to Star's, and headed to the food. Rowan was tense, he could tell from across the room. She, he noted, was not belting her oms, but quietly singing. The only proof of her participation was a rise in her shoulders every once in awhile.

Elbow to elbow, the troops sat, some having to hold their plates in their laps in order to eat off of them. There was lots of eye rolling and silent disgust throughout dinner. Too soon, the dinner crew sat up and started clearing dishes. Finally, calm settled over the diners, only to be shattered with the evening's crude play. Tonight though, the thespians had wigs and full costumes.

The theme of the play was clearly aimed at Rowan, and it was not kind. After a few rounds of, 'oh no what are we to do?' one of the actors came out dressed as a queen and started shouting ridiculous commands at them, 'color the sky pink,' 'dress only in rainbow colors,' 'always, always stay together, even when going to the bathroom'.

Mercilessly, the play ended with, "Change is the Only Constant." A sentiment completely opposite of the theme itself, which only showed the passive aggressive nature of the entire exercise. Shane saw how clever that was; now if someone called them out on being negative, they would all claim the play to be in support while still spilling their true feelings.

An uneasy quiet settled back over the room as the crew scrambled off to pass out the dessert plates. Just as Shane finished his apple crumble, Star slipped him a note. Opening it under the table, he almost coughed as he read the three little words on the paper, 'come over tonight?' *Persistent, isn't she.*

When all the plates seemed to have emptied and a stillness took hold of the room, he waited as the air crackled. Shane didn't know what the tension was all about, but he could feel it. Suddenly, Jolly got up with a loud bang, his fist hitting the table.

"Some of you think you know everything," he opened, walking up to the center of the room. The diners facing away from him all turned their chairs toward him.

"You people think you have it all figured out. You all have reached a minuscule amount of awareness and now you're flying high on your arrogance. Let me tell you people, the fastest way back down is pride. Hubris. The Greeks knew it well..."

Jolly continued to talk about the dangers of pride, arrogance and hubris for another hour and a half. Shane wanted to put a gun to his own head before the evening was over. Maybe that was his secret power over them: this was enough to make the most stubborn person admit to anything just to get the guy to shut the hell up.

Finally, and without warning, Jolly turned in midsentence and walked out of the room. Shane had stopped listening long ago and had no idea what caused his sudden departure, but he was thankful nonetheless. His eyes glanced around the room and landed on Jewel and Colt. Colt looked nothing like he thought he would: long, blonde hair, slight beard, muscular but weak at the same time, as if his life force couldn't fill up his body.

Jewel was exactly the way he had pictured her. Her light green eyes spit evil wherever they landed, with a touch of sexual prowess that both promised a night of passion and scared the crap out of any man who dared ask for it.

She rose and turned to Colt expectantly, waiting for him to join her. Without hesitation he jumped up and followed her out, head down, shoulders slumped forward. Shane couldn't help but shake his head. Poor sod, having to live with that after Rowan.

His eyes flew to Rowan in time to see her stand and depart the same way Jewel and Colt did. Only she walked slowly, gracefully, with her head held high and her shoulders back. He hoped she would look back his way one more time, but she never did, just walked right out the door into the night.

"Well?" Star asked him, pulling his attention back.

"Here's the thing Star, I like you, but it's just not going to happen that way." He leveled with her, figuring she was never going to give up.

Undeterred, she ran her hands through his hair, "Well, if you change your mind, you know where I'll be. Right outside your door."

Gritting his teeth, her touch so unlike Rowan's he could barely stand it, he waited while she had her fun before walking away pouting.

"Dude, you hit that yet?" Beck walked up behind him.

"No, Beck. I haven't hit that yet. And I won't, not that desperate. I like to have a little connection with the women I sleep with."

"Oh, listen to the hubris on that one!" Beck hollered, bringing everyone's attention to their conversation. Shane was really starting to hate Beck.

"Yeah, Beck, that's exactly how to use that word. Nice one!" Shane said before walking back to the sanctuary of his own room.

• • •

She just didn't understand the reception she was getting. She thought everyone would like what she was doing. Hadn't she heard the grumblings about the new routine? No one liked the separate meetings and dinners. No one liked the gross training exercises. If she was going to stay here and give up her dreams— her life, she was going to do something good. She'd heard them and was trying to fix it, but it felt as if everyone was about to revolt. This had never happened to her before.

Truth be told, she always worked with kids so the

entire group never really cared that much about what she did or the changes she had made, but still. She'd heard the comments as she was leaving, listened to the complaints about her arrogance and style, caught the way they looked at her. As if she was crazy.

Throwing herself on her bed, she wondered where she went wrong. Honestly, she didn't care about any of this. Didn't they understand that? She was sacrificing her life to makes things better for them, her whole life! If she had her druthers, she'd go back to her old life where people just left her alone. The Snack Shack seemed like a luxury now, whining teenagers and all.

What she would do to be able to go back to Fresh Greens. Tears sprang into her eyes as she thought about her old life. She hated it here. No matter what she did, someone was mad, someone hated what she was doing, someone was waiting for her to fail. And now she was left with no one, feeling sorry for herself, back to wishing for another life. Almost as if she had come full circle.

Feeling the breeze against her skin alerted her to the window opening. Shane. Sitting up, she waited for him. She didn't know how, but somehow he had found his way back into her room. She got up and checked the lock on her door. When she came back to her bed Shane was sitting on it.

"Don't you look like the cat that ate the canary."

"So, what was he talking about tonight? I mean, does it really take over two hours to say, 'hey people, you're all getting a little too big for your own britches. Snap the fuck out of it?'"

She laughed in spite of herself. "I know, right? I thought tonight would never end."

She plopped down next to him, happy for the company, anything to get out of her own head. He wrapped his arm around her and pulled her close, breathing in her scent.

"I hate to tell you this, lady, but your friends are fucked up," he told her, smiling in her hair.

She laughed again, this time feeling the tears spill over onto her cheeks. "You could say that again."

"Baby, don't cry. I'm right here. Come here." He wrapped himself around her, cocooning her. It felt so good to be enveloped in him. She inhaled his smell, feeling his warmth bring her back to life.

"I'm not crying, I'm just—I don't know. I just don't get it here anymore."

"Did you ever?"

Locking eyes with him, she smiled a sad smile, "No, I never really did."

Brushing the hair from her eyes, Shane kissed her, waking her insides and warming her heart, confusing her more. Kissing him back, she reached for his shirt. In this moment, she wanted nothing more than to crawl back into her bubble with Shane. Guilt flooded her system; she was using him, she knew that now. There was no future for them but when she was with him, the rest of the world faded away, leaving nothing but Shane and bliss. Right now she needed both.

He stood and pulled off his jeans while toeing off his shoes. Something seemed off in his movements, but she brushed it aside. She did the same while watching him disrobe. The work he had been doing was starting to make changes to his body. Now it was chiseled as if an artist had created him. His shoulders bulged while his arm muscles moved as he ripped off his pants.

Her mouth watered as she watched his fingers push down his cotton briefs, unleashing his hard cock. Before she knew it, he was helping her undress. Almost pushing her to the bed, slipping down her jeans, unsnapping her bra, pulling off her panties, leaving her naked and wanting.

He climbed on top of her, his knee pushing her thigh open, memories of every time he had done that exact move flooding her brain. She became slick when his mouth clamped down hard on her pebbled nipple. His hands smoothed down her side, claiming her from shoulder to hip.

His entire body moved up and down hers, titillating her skin as his hard muscles rubbed her. She could feel his cock sliding over her stomach, getting closer and closer to her center as he slipped his body over hers. The weight of him made her head explode.

"Oh, Rowan, I miss you so much. I can't live without you," he moaned in her ear, his voice strained, his tongue sliding along her neck.

"Please," she begged him. For what, exactly, she didn't know.

Lifting his hips, he centered himself at her core and pushed in hard. The electricity flowed into her the lower he sank; soon she would be able to light the room. He was more aggressive than she had ever remembered, yet restrained at the same time. Or maybe that was just projection. Shame slithered up her spine. Never had she felt so conflicted before. She knew this was wrong, but never needed anything so badly in her life. And right then she remembered that she would do anything for this man. This man opened a world she didn't know existed before and with him it lay at her feet.

Her eyes flew to his, locking his stare. She tried to convey her feelings to him, but again the look on his face blew her away. He seemed lost, tortured and in ecstasy at the same time. She watched him as he started moving his hips faster, sinking into her over and over again. Sweat formed along his hair line as he exhaled deeply.

"I love you, Rowan. Don't ever forget that."

"I love you, Shane. I'll never forget," it flew out of her mouth on its own volition. Aghast at her admission, she pushed up on her elbows and kissed him to keep her mouth shut.

He deepened the kiss while growling in her mouth. Her hips pushed into his, causing him to go deeper, hitting that spot she loved so much. Faster, harder, he slammed into her, his weight taking her breath from her.

Letting her head fall back and opening wider for him seemed to entice him more. He let go of all restraint, pumping into her at an inhuman pace. Soon she was overcome with pleasure, her orgasm silently taking hold, her wide smile the only outward sign of the firestorm of pleasure wracking her body.

Growling not so softly, his movements became sporadic as his own release overwhelmed his muscles, taking control, until he collapsed on top of her.

She felt him move to get up, but she couldn't bear to be left alone. Holding him close to her, he settled back down next to her, holding her in return. She snuggled back into him creating a perfect spoon. He pulled the covers over them before the blackness pulled her under.

CHAPTER FOURTEEN

Nothing was going her way, and Shane was starting to feel bad, but was more convinced than ever that this was the only way. Truth be told, his sole focus was getting Rowan out of here and free of Jolly. Would he like to free all of these people? Without question. Was he concerned about the kids on the property? Absolutely. One thing at a time. Rowan first, then the kids. The rest of these assholes could rot here. Even with Justin's explanation, he still didn't understand how they could watch what was happening here and not call the authorities. Had they lost their basic humanity?

He watched day after day as Rowan tried and failed to connect with the people here. He found it easier and easier to manipulate the people around him, dropping hints here and there about her greedy desires to take over, about her instability, about her being out of touch with reality. He found it almost fascinating how quickly people adopted those opinions as their own.

Storm's reaction to the whole affair was the most amusing to him. Having nothing but ill will toward the woman, he was infinitely entertained by her attempts to stop a coup that ultimately did not exist. He guessed

Jolly never really shared his full expectation of Rowan's role with her. She seemed just as shocked as everyone else as Rowena seemingly usurped control of the group.

Every time he'd ask Rowan to leave with him, she would throw the unprotected children in his face. How could she leave them again, look what happened last time? They took their food away—how could he ask her to abandon them? She was right, but that didn't change the fact that she needed to leave with him. This was the puzzle Shane had been working out over the last few hours. How could he get Rowan to leave willingly and protect the children?

He needed reinforcements. He needed a phone and was just working out how to get hold of one when he was interrupted.

"Yo, Shane," Fern called him over.

Damn. He walked over to where Fern stood with Storm and Beck.

"When was the last time you met with Rowena?" Storm's sharp voice stabbed at him.

Last night. "I don't know, we only met once or twice."

"She just made a request and before I grant it, I wanted to see if anyone had met with her lately. She seems much more stable now, but I know in private you said she was really showing signs of incoherence."

Shane had never told anyone she was incoherent, but he didn't correct her. He had no information to add. "What request?"

"Just looking into old records. But given how strangely she's been acting, I wanted to ask if you've seen her."

"Nope. I can ask to see her, if that would help you?"

Storm looked at him, her eyes narrowing. He knew

she could sense his insincerity, but couldn't put her finger on it. Shane knew how to act and had been undercover plenty of times before; although he had let his true feelings slip out every once in a while, these days he had a pretty good handle on it. Who could blame him though, with how fucked up things were around here?

"That might be a good idea. I'll set it up."

With that, Storm turned and marched off. Shane glanced up at Beck.

"I hope you know what you're doing," Beck warned him, "Rowena might be a little off these days, but I know she has a sharp mind and an unforgiving nature. Don't let those big brown eyes fool you, she's just as ruthless as Jewel. Only worse, cause she hides behind her innocence."

"Whoa, sounds like a story, Beck. What she do, take your teddy bear when you were kids?"

Beck scowled at him, "Rowena was never a kid."

Confused, Shane watched Beck march away from him. Completely baffled. That was the most common feeling living here. Plain baffled.

Back to the problem at hand; he needed a phone.

• • •

Walking into the conference room, she knew something was amiss. It was the middle of the day and everyone should have been on their afternoon crews, but instead they had all gathered for this meeting. Swallowing hard on the memories of all the times she walked into this very room on a mission for someone else. Her son, her friends, her school. Now she walked in with no mission, no one to fight for, no role to play—just herself.

She was surprised to see who was gathered at the table: Cheri, Jewel, Colt, and Jolly to name a few. Conspicuously absent were Storm and Eden, or anyone from Storm's private inner circle of loyal followers.

"Rowena, come in child. Have a seat." Jolly's voice was sticky sweet, never a good sign.

"So, what's going on?" she asked the table, trying to hide fear.

"You suck as a leader, that's what going on," Jewel piped up, causing a ripple of inhales across the room.

"Jewel," Jolly gave her warning, "Rowena, it seems you are not as ready for this role as I had hoped you'd be. I'm thinking it might be wise for you to step back."

"Step back?" Rowan asked. She glanced around the table looking at their faces. Did everyone here know how she was forced back here? Or did they think she wanted this? That she begged Jewel to let her back in?

"Everyone here knows the importance of your part as a role model, however symbolic that is," Jolly started to say.

"Symbolic?" she asked, interrupting him.

"I just think that maybe you took on too much too soon. Maybe in a little while you can go back to working on the dharma, but for now let's let Storm and Eden worry about all that," Cheri spoke to her as if to a child.

All at once it became clear what was happening. They did think she had asked to come back, they did think she made a deal with the devil to take her place as a bona fide leader. How could any of them believe that? Colt and Jewel forced her to come. Jolly drugged her and kept her locked up for weeks. Cheri was her guard, for God's sake. Humiliation crept up her neck.

Truth be told, she tried and failed to do what Jolly wanted of her. And now he didn't know what to do with her. She would be cast aside and left to rot. Just when she thought she could create something good out of her God awful life, even that was stripped from her.

Nodding her head, she agreed with Cheri. "Was there anything else?"

"Yes, that new recruit, Shane, has asked to see you again. You seem to have a magic touch with him. Maybe your role will be working with newbies, getting them settled. God knows Star's charms seem to have failed with this one."

Her head snapped up at the mention of Shane's name. Why would he ask to see her? Just drawing more attention to himself and their connection. She nodded her assent and got up to leave. As she left the room, she heard them start talking about her again. How she had lost her touch, how disappointing her performance had been. How bad the streets must have been to have caused such madness.

Madness. The word stuck in her throat and rolled around her head. Madness is having your life ripped from you. Madness is having someone threaten your son over and over again. Madness is being forced to do the one thing you swore you would never do again. Yeah, she was mad all right.

~

She waited for Shane in the library, noticing that now that she was declared a failure, no one was watching her. Jolly had won; he brought her back, convinced her that this was what she wanted, and then watched her fall apart. She was broken, which was exactly where he wanted her to be in the first place. She wondered if this was his plan all along. Revenge for defying him so many years ago.

Shane walked in and sat without speaking. Moving to sit across from him, she waited.

"Things have changed," she spoke first, "I am no longer on a watch list. Look," she got up and shut the door. No one came by and opened it. They waited for a full five minutes before daring to speak again. "According to the powers that be, I'm not worthy enough to take on leadership responsibilities just yet."

Shane laughed out loud.

"And you're laughing?"

"Damn right I'm laughing. The only question is, why aren't you?"

Rowan did not see what was so funny about it. Her entire life was one big failure after another.

"Rowan, don't you see the irony? All this time Jolly has been telling everyone who would listen that you were the answer to everything. That you would lead this group to the next level and save everyone on the planet or some other big heap of horse shit. And it was all going to happen by what, next month? He commits some serious felonies to get you back and then his people reject you! Come on, that's the best way this story could end!"

She started to laugh a little. It was pretty funny when she thought about it like that. It wasn't she who failed, it was Jolly—all of this was his doing. He brought her here, insisted on her taking on this stupid role, and the people here wanted nothing to do with her.

Soon she was laughing just as hard as he was, wiping away the tears flowing out of her eyes and holding her stomach. After a few minutes, she pulled herself together.

"So, now what?" she asked as he sat up in the chair.

"Good question. You requested some records, tell me about them."

She didn't want to know how he knew that, but she was impressed anyway.

"I was going over the old budgets to compare them to what we are doing now. The records room is locked up pretty tight, but I wanted to see Lina's budgets. Find more money for them. Why?"

"Are everyone's legal names on those documents?"

"Not on the budgets, but if I get access to the record's room, I can get them. Where are you going with this?"

Shane sat up, all signs of laughter and amusement gone. "Are you ready to shut this place down and come home?"

Her breath stopped. Shut this place down? As in no more community? No more Jolly?

"Ro, I need you to answer me. Jolly has destroyed enough lives. He won't leave you alone, even though it appears you don't have what it takes to please him and his people. You won't leave without protecting the kids here and I won't leave without you. Our only option is to take him out."

"You're going kill him?" she whispered in horror.

Shane couldn't help but smirk at her, "No. I'm not going to kill anyone. Can you get a list of legal names? I'll do the rest."

Suddenly, thoughts of escape reentered her mind. Was it possible? Could she really escape, for good this time? Could she live her life her way and protect her family? Without leaving the kids vulnerable?

She nodded and couldn't stop the smile spreading across her face.

"That's my girl. Welcome back, Ro! I've missed you." Shane got up and kissed her right on the mouth before walking out.

Looking around the library, everything seemed a

little brighter, a little better. Hope. She realized she had hope again. Walking out trying to contain her excitement, she bit her lip and forced a worried expression onto her face, but she felt like she was floating.

Which is exactly why she didn't see Cheri when she walked into her room.

"You look pretty happy."

Rowan darn near screamed, but held her hand to her heart, almost jumping out of her skin instead, "Jesus. You scared the crap out of me. What are you doing here?"

"Cleaning," Cheri answered brightly.

"Why? I thought now that I was allowed to be up and about I could clean my own room."

"It seems that you might want me around. You know," Cheri paused, "some friendships last a long time. I still remember palling around with Talia as kids. We were a lot like you and Lina. I have to say that after you and Talia left, we've become quite close."

Rowan knew there was some sort of secret code in there, but for the life of her she could not make out what.

"Um, okay," was all she could think of to say.

Cheri waited, then turned and went back to cleaning the room. Just as she was leaving, she turned to Rowan, "You never know where you're going to find your best friends, ya know. I'll be cleaning your room for a while yet, so if you ever need anything, you just let me know."

Again, Rowan could tell there was a secret message, but couldn't decode it. She nodded and Cheri left her alone.

CHAPTER FIFTEEN

He'd been waiting in the dark for over thirty minutes and finally felt like he was ready. Slipping into the hall, he meandered toward the house phone. After watching for days he knew where the cords were kept and when the traffic would be the least. Everyone should be in their afternoon crews, but he learned early that not everyone actually followed this so called dharma, lots of the higher ups tended to more important things. Funny how the more important tasks were never the manual labor everyone else was required to do.

It was time to call in reinforcements. He'd been there long enough and was pretty sure Rob and Cody were about to break down the doors looking for him. While he wanted their help, he was hoping for a little more finesse. This wasn't his first rodeo, but the stakes felt higher this time. If he got caught he'd be kicked out, leaving Rowan alone.

Looking as nonchalant as he could as his heart pounded in his chest, he walked up to the locked linen closet next to the table that housed the phone, a vase of flowers and photos of Jolly in various places. Taking out his tools, he popped the lock and reached in, hoping like hell the phone cord was still there.

Luck was on his side. His fingers grasped the cord, neatly coiled and tucked right where it should be. Locking the closet and tucking his prize in his pocket, he walked out, head down, hoping to appear lost in thought.

Heading straight to the Deck House, his heart rate ticked up with the adrenaline flowing in his blood. Last time he made it this far, he had no idea that the bastards left the phones out, but hid the cords. Now he had the damn cord, all he needed was a little luck and an empty Deck House.

Shivering slightly with the memories of Saturday Exercise, he opened the door and snuck up the stairs. He'd refused to participate in any more training and hadn't been in the Arena except the one time to find the phone. From what he had heard, they had toned down the violence and Jewel had been forbidden from using animals. Still, just walking across the Arena made his skin crawl. He swiftly made it to the base of the stairs and leapt up them two at time.

He waited, listening, hoping. After a full seven minutes of stillness, he decided it was safe and continued up the stairs, opening the door and glancing around before getting to work. He locked the door behind him, no sense in giving them a free pass to find him. Making quick work of running the phone cord from the jack to the phone, he angled himself under the desk near the window, just in case.

He almost shouted in relief when he heard that precious dial tone, but held himself in check. Dialing Rob first, he almost prayed for him to answer. It rang five times and went to voicemail. *Shit. No good.* Dialing Cody next, he felt the need to throw up just before the call connected.

"Yo, this is Cody."

"Thank Fuck. I'm so glad to hear your voice."

"Shane? Where the fuck are you?" Cody asked, sounding genuinely worried.

"Hiding in the fucking Deck House. I need—"

"What the fuck, man? Do they not have phones there? You were supposed to call in two weeks ago?" Cody interrupted him.

"Easy, Grandma. And no, asshole, they don't have phones here. You have no idea what it took just to get this one. You and Rob need to come in for the extraction plan. Bring a phone, they won't search you—I don't think. I know where to stash some stuff. Get here."

"10-4. Justin wants to know—"

"Yeah, she's fine. A little shaky about how to go forward, but getting better every day. Tell him she'll see him soon."

"Got it. Hang tight."

Shane hung up and felt almost buoyant knowing his partners were on their way. Close, they were so close to getting out of here.

He picked up the phone one more time and dialed a different number, hoping like hell he was making the right call.

• • •

"Rowena?" Cheri's voice on the other side of her door startled her.

"Yeah?" Rowan opened the door after having caught her breath.

"So! Just got word that you now have access to the records room. It officially starts tomorrow but we still have a bit of time before dinner, thought we could go check it out." She stood in the doorway, jangling the key in her hand.

At first she was elated she had been granted access, but then Rowan hesitated on the threshold, not sure what to say.

"No time like the present, Ro. Let's go." Cheri's voice turned sharp and Rowan nodded her assent without further thought.

Following her quick pace out of the building, Rowan couldn't help but wonder what this was all about it. Afternoon crew was just ending and everyone should be finishing up and starting to prepare for dinner. Why on earth would Cheri want to start this now? Rowan needed to be alone in the room, not with her ever present guard.

Walking into the private offices, she felt as if she was trespassing. She had never been allowed access to this part of the building. Cheri gleefully opened each door they passed through, carefully locking it behind them. The hallways were empty and the offices were dark. Clearly, they were the only ones around.

They passed Jewel's office and Rowan held back the urge to vandalize it. Smiling at her adolescent thoughts, she trotted to keep up with Cheri. Finally coming to a stop at the end of the long hall, Cheri once again took out her key and opened the door.

The room was much bigger than Rowan had expected, rows and rows of filing cabinets lined the walls and boxes were stacked to the ceiling above them. Each box was labeled with a number and a color and the cabinets were marked with a combination of letters.

"So, this is the records room," Cheri told her brightly.

"I can see that."

"As you can see, everything is coded and you need

the master list to find anything. I happen to know where it is. I thought I'd line you out on how all this works and that way if I'm still busy with morning work, you don't have to wait for me. The key is yours."

Cheri gingerly laid it on the table. Rowan swallowed hard as she realized the implication of that gesture. She was just handed the key to everything she needed and Cheri just told her she would be alone tomorrow morning.

"Thank you," Rowan said, her voice suddenly weak with appreciation.

"Here is how this whole thing works. You find the list in this first drawer and look for the topic you need," she pulled open a filing cabinet and pulled out a large bundle of papers. "So, let's say you wanted to look up birth records. You just find birth and look for the code. Looks like the last five years of birth records are in the box labeled TMY and anything past that is in the pale yellow 845 cabinet. So just find that box or that cabinet. See?"

She walked further into the room and found TMY and then pointed up and found the correctly marked box.

"Got it. Simple enough."

"These are all the records, the cold storage has all the videotapes, cassette recordings, and photos. Along with some other old stuff of Jolly's. That's housed under the Arena." Cheri went on with her explanation as Rowan nodded her head. "I think you'll find what you're looking for in here."

Cheri gave her that look again and for the life of Rowan, she could not figure out what secret message she was supposed to understand.

"Well, look at that! I need to take off. Why don't you

stick around and try to look up some stuff before dinner, that way you'll be ready to rock and roll tomorrow."

Before Rowan even had time to ask a question or agree to stay, Cheri was gone. She was alone. Taking a deep breath, she grabbed the list and looked up the corporate board files. Of course it wasn't that easy and she had to remember what they were called, but after searching for a few minutes she found what she was looking for.

Marching down to file number 348, she opened the drawer and fingered through each folder. Finally she pulled the file and opened it. Her heart flew into her chest. Page one was what she was looking for. A complete list of all the board members' full, legal names. And Jolly's was right there on top. Ronald J. Mayfield, Director of Development.

A quick search of the other boards and companies all confirmed that Ronald J. Mayfield was the Director of Development for most of them. On a few he was listed as CEO, but mostly he held the same title for everything. The only part she didn't understand was the duplicate lists labeled, 'Civil List'. On those lists, he was listed as Jolly Mayfield and some other names were deleted all together.

She couldn't wait to tell Shane. A smile swept over her face—Shane. Her last thought each night, her first thought every morning. She didn't know what his plan was, but she knew that she trusted him. The thought made her freeze; she actually trusted him with everything, her heart, her soul, her life. For the first time she felt absolutely loved and cared for. With Shane here, nothing could touch her. She just needed to stop drawing attention to herself and get the records he needed.

Rowan had no idea how long she'd been in the records room and was worried she would be late for dinner. She put everything back as neatly as she could with shaky hands and fled.

CHAPTER SIXTEEN

"No, you can't take their food money! Those are kids down there, not just the teachers, and it wasn't the teachers that over spent on the construction." Rowan was shouting across the table while everyone else just sat there as if they were robots.

"The teachers over spent on curriculum, not construction. They are out of money. What's done is done." Jewel's icy voice grated over her nerves, making her see red.

"I cannot even believe this is even a topic of discussion. Food is food. Not optional. If you want to restrict their supply budget, construction budget, fine. But not food. And for the record, they did over spend on construction and they were not managing that project."

Rowan knew that budget by heart. She had been assigned the task of budgetary monitor — what ever that even meant. She suspected it was Jewel. With Rowan down in the records room all day, every day, Jewel had free reign to do as she pleased without Rowan pestering her. Now that she had been working in the records room for over a week, she was expected to know the ins and outs of each budget and show up to every dreaded meeting anyone had about money. It was a nightmare.

And to top it off, Jewel was once again suggesting that Lina's operating budget be cut. The only items in the operating budget were food, gas, and electricity. No supplies, no toys, no books, nothing. These people were seriously discussing the pros and cons of cutting off food for children. Some of them were parents—it was atrocious.

"Where is Lina, anyway?" Rowan asked.

"Lina is not invited to these meetings," Jewel snapped at her.

Even better. The school's director wasn't even allowed to participate in her own budget meetings. Rowan was ready to throw all of these people to the wolves. It had been days since she handed over Jolly's real name with no word on what the next step would be. Her frustration level was through the roof.

"I, for one, believe strongly that Lina should be present when we are discussing her school," Rowan said through clenched teeth.

Silence filled the room. What little power Rowan had left was rapidly deteriorating. Most of time these meetings lasted no more than fifteen minutes and people were annoyed. But then, most of them did not propose cutting food for children.

"I believe that we need to reschedule this for another time," Eden finally spoke up, breaking the tension filling the room.

"And let's please schedule it with Lina in mind. She should be here," Rowan jumped back in.

"You've made your point, Rowena. Now you need to let it go," Storm about growled at her before getting up, signifying the end of the meeting.

Rowan watched as the zombies filed out of the

room. What was wrong with everybody? Did they not see how absolutely insane this entire process was? Soon she was alone in the conference room and she sat wondering how much longer she was going to have to deal with all this madness before Shane's plan was ready to go. Not long, she hoped.

She needed to find Lina. They hardly saw each other now that Rowan was back. Rising from her chair, she wondered how much Lina knew about what was happening. Did she know that the powers that be were cutting her budget, halting her construction project, and holding back food?

The more she thought about it, the more infuriated she became. She stormed out of the building and headed down to the Instructary. She noticed a commotion by the Big House. New recruits getting settled. No matter how messed up this place got, more people just kept showing up. Rowan shook her head and kept her pace down the path.

Sneaking into the classroom as to not disturb anyone, Rowan was surprised to find the classroom in what looked like complete pandemonium. Several easels lined the wall by the windows, blocks and Legos littered the rug in the center of the room, and the dress up corner looked as if a bomb went off near it, dresses, scarfs, hats, coats, and a variety of unidentified clothing lying every which way.

The kids were everywhere all at once. Three of the older kids seemed to be painting a large group canvas while the little ones darted back and forth between the chaos on the rug and the chaos in the dress up area. The noise level was out of control with kids squealing, laughing, and shouting to one another.

Rowan looked around for Lina, or one of the other teachers, but found no one over the age of twelve.

Making her way over to the bigger kids, she stepped past the mess and continued her search for an adult.

"Hi," she shouted at one of the boys, "Where's Lina?"

"Lina's in the back cooking lunch for us. We're in charge," the boy answered proudly.

"Okay, thanks." Rowan made her way back across the sea of debris and headed back to the kitchen.

When she walked in her heart broke a little. Lina was working quickly, getting lunch together. A large bowl of rice and beans sat on the stove while a small pile of carrots sat on the counter as she chopped. There were trays ready to go with small glasses of water all gathered at the edge of the counter.

Lina's hair was tied up on her head, showing her full profile. She looked gaunt with deep purple under her eyes.

"Lina! Where are your teachers or helpers?"

Her head popped up and she smiled, "Rowan! Hi. Hold on and I can visit with you. I just need to get this lunch set up first."

"Lina, why are you alone down here?" Rowan asked, as she jumped in to help. She knew the drill, helped to create the drill, actually.

Without answering, Lina handed over the knife and went to work on gathering bowls and silverware. Rowan immediately saw how she reorganized the kitchen, to have the kids start helping in here, she presumed. It was obvious that Lina had been alone for a while and seemed to be moving stiffly with exhaustion.

The two of them finished the lunch prep and Lina went back out to get the kids. Soon all the kids had large helpings of beans and rice in their bowls and small plates of carrots. Rowan watched as Lina pulled aside the three older children and spoke to them. They nodded and went back to their lunch.

Seemingly satisfied, Lina came back to Rowan in the kitchen and lead her outside to the play yard. Without speaking, they walked through the yard and straight back to the shed. It was only after they were inside that Lina finally turned and spoke to her.

"They took everyone. I'm it. They said my budget is overdrawn and unless I wanted to go without food—again—I had to give up my teachers. There were only three of us down here to begin with, but man, now I'm completely alone." Lina's eyes were wide with emotion.

"When? The meeting wasn't even until this morning?"

"A few days ago. Marley and Shasta try to sneak back down here just before dinner and then at bedtime to help. Plus, they still have rooms down here, but all day, I'm it. And the kids can feel it, they know something isn't right. The little ones aren't sleeping well and the older ones are acting out."

"Jesus. That's what I came down to talk to you about. We just had a budget meeting. Jewel, Storm, Eden, me, and a few others all talking about your school—without you. They never said it already happened. I guess they figured everyone would just agree like always."

"I know, they already told me I have no money for more food. Don't worry, I hid a few sacks of beans after last time. The kids are going to get sick of it, but it's better than nothing."

"Lina. This is crazy. This isn't right." Rowan waited, she wanted to say more, but Lina looked like she was going to crack if she said anything else.

"Ro. I'm surviving hour by hour down here. You do

what you need to, but until things settle down, I can't work on anything with you. I like your spirit, though. Looks like you made it back to your old self."

Rowan nodded her head. She knew what she was saying. Who has time or energy to plan a revolution when you can barely get through each day? She hugged her and turned to leave.

"Lina," she turned back at the last minute. "Hang in there. I promise, I'm going to fix this."

Rowan turned and marched back up the hill to find Storm. Storm knew that Lina had already been stripped of her help and her budget during that meeting and never said a word. The powers that be believed that everyone sitting at that table were zombies and would just agree to the new budget. So much so that a few days ago they already started laying down the new law. *A few days ago!*

What was the point of gathering in that stifling room and voting? What was the point of her life if it was to oversee budgets that did not exist or would be overruled by Storm and Jewel regardless of what anyone else said or did?

She went to Storm's office first, but found it empty. Undeterred, she turned around and went straight to the Big House. Once inside, she heard voices coming from the living room. Rounding the corner, she almost fainted at the site of Cody standing in the center of the room with another man who looked vaguely familiar talking to Eden and Storm.

Eden noticed her first, "Oh perfect. This is our Welcoming Ambassador, Rowena."

Her head snapped around on that one. Welcoming Ambassador, really? That was new to her, but she let it go. She needed to talk to Storm, and now.

"Hello everyone. Welcome aboard. Storm, can we

chat, now?" Rowan's smile was tight and her voice had an edge she was tired of hiding.

"Rowena! It's Sam." Sam pulled himself away from the group and enveloped her in a large hug.

"Sam? Oh my God. I didn't even recognize you. Hi!" Rowan said from deep within his arms.

"Have you seen Lina?" Sam whispered in her ear. Rowan nodded her head before he broke his grip and stepped back.

"Yes, it's great to see you, Sam. Same place as always, ya know. I always see you in the same place," Rowan spoke, hoping Sam would catch her code. "And you might be?" She extended her hand to Cody.

"I'm Cody. Nice to meet you, Rowena, is it? I was lucky enough to meet Sam on the road and he brought me here. Everyone is just so nice," Cody said to the group.

So this was Shane's plan, bring in Cody? She didn't quite see how getting another person stuck here would be a good thing, but right at this moment, she didn't have time to think about it. She needed to talk to Storm about getting Lina some help.

"So Storm, you didn't mention this morning that you had already shifted Marley and Shasta from the Instructary, leaving Lina completely alone with almost twenty kids."

Sam straightened up at that and she heard Storm inhale.

"We can talk about that later, Rowena. Right now we're getting the new people settled," Storm interjected.

"New people?" Rowan started, "I've know Sam my whole life. I'd hardly call him new. Welcome back, by the way. I'm sure Lina could use your help down in the Instructary, her other teachers have been reassigned."

"Rowena, why don't you come with me and let Storm get Sam and Cody settled?" Eden said while walking across the room toward her.

Surprised, Rowan stared at her. Eden hadn't spoken to her since her return. Come to think of it, Eden hadn't spoken directly to her for years.

"I hardly think the Instructary is an appropriate placement for you two. I think the first order of business is to get you squared away with some rooms," Storm was saying as Eden led Rowan out of the room.

Snapping out of it, she tried to pull out of Eden's grip and found her strength surprising. Without a word, Eden marched them down the hall and into her room. Soon Rowan felt like she was ten years old, in trouble for some unknown travesty.

"I am so ashamed of you," Eden spit out as she shoved her into the room.

"What? You're ashamed of me?"

"Look at you. Mouthing off in front of recruits. To Storm, no less. You have wasted everything I ever gave you."

Rowan stood still, letting Eden's words wash over her.

"All I ever wanted was to live my own life—my way," Rowan told her, after a few minutes.

"Your way? The opportunities you squandered. The choices you made. You had everything handed to you on a golden platter and you threw it in our faces."

"Are you seriously talking about that right now? I was twelve years old. Out there in the real world, people go to jail for what you wanted me to do. Jail!" Rowan screamed at her. After all this time, she was still upset at her mother for not protecting her.

"Well, it sure didn't stop you from jumping in bed

with someone else. And of all people. I was trying to keep you from turning into a classic American slut. We could all see that that's where you were headed. Marrying Jolly would have saved your life. He was doing you a favor," Eden hissed at her, her eyes wide with rage.

Rowan stopped moving, barely breathing, and took in the woman before her. Did she honestly think all this time that Jolly was helping her? That he wasn't some creepy sex offender? That Jolly never hit her or threatened her?

"A favor?" she whispered, "You think Jolly was doing me a favor?" She shook her head. "I was happy. I had friends and Lina and I had plans. We wanted to grow up and make the world a better place. We wanted to go out in the world and tell everyone who would listen to come live here and join Jolly. That Jolly would make the world the way it should be. I believed everything he ever told me."

Eden blew out a long breath and smoothed out her short, grey hair.

"I protected myself from him. He's a monster. No man in their right mind wants to marry a twelve year old. It's wrong and you should have protected me."

"For the record, you were a mature teenager. Jolly is not a monster. I don't always understand his methods, but I have faith in him. I wouldn't be here without him. Where was your faith?"

"My faith?" Rowan almost laughed. "I had every ounce of faith until he wanted to have sex with me. Even back then I knew that wasn't right. And now, after having lived a few years in the real world, I know for sure it was wrong. How many others, Eden? How many babies have you sent his way? In the name of The Work, or Faith, or tutoring? How many, Mom?"

"You're crazy. Weak and crazy. Jolly is a great man and would never hurt anyone. He does what he does because he has to. You think he likes it? You think he wants to keep up the teachings, over and over again? You people need to try harder. He's only one man and you people are sucking him dry. He's a great man."

"What the hell are you talking about? And I'm the crazy one?"

Rowan paced the room, hoping to calm down. Her blood was pumping behind her ears and she could feel her face hot with humiliation and shame. She knew what her mother said was wrong, insane even, but it still hurt. How little did her own mother think of her?

"I've done everything I can with you. I washed my hands of you the day you took off." Eden sat down and stared at the ceiling, signifying the end of their conversation.

"Well, mom. We should do this again. It reminds me of all the reasons why I protected Justin the way I did. He's great, by the way, really smart, kind, protective and loyal. I guess he got those traits from his dad's side." Rowan spun on her heel and walked out, leaving Eden alone.

CHAPTER SEVENTEEN

Tired, muddy, and grumpy, Shane walked into the Big House looking forward to a hot shower and a hot meal. He was not looking forward to another long dinner with a bizarre themed play. He was about done with the shenanigans of living here. Even treating it like a case, he could barely get through each day.

Walking in, he heard voices in the living room and wondered what was happening. Most of the time, this place was quiet as a church—he'd come to hate it. Rounding the corner, he came face to face with Cody.

Beck was talking about the crew he'd be joining in the morning and Cody was nodding his head enthusiastically.

"Shane, I'd like you to meet the newest member of our team," Beck said as he approached the pair.

He stuck his hand out and greeted Cody, "Nice to meet you."

"I'm Cody. Just arrived this afternoon with Sam. We were traveling together and stopped here for a bit. Looks like we're staying a while. I'd love to jump in and help where I can." Cody shook his hand, smiling.

Shane felt muscles relax for the first time in months. Cody was here. Thank Fuck.

"Oh, yeah? Where you from?" Shane asked, barely able to contain his laughter.

"Ohio, but I've been traveling a long time now."

"And Sam? Who's he?"

"Just someone I met on the road. He's around here someplace. Said he knew a place we could crash."

There was more to that story, but Shane would have to wait to hear it. He could hear the dinner crew start up and knew he didn't have much time to clean up for dinner.

"Well, I gotta run and get ready for the evening meal. It's a great experience. You'll love it." Shane raised his eyebrows at Cody and turned to leave. He couldn't wait for Cody to sit through his first dinner. It would take everything in his power not to fall out of his chair laughing watching Cody experience it.

~

Clean and a lot less grumpy, Shane walked into the dining room looking for Cody. After the disaster dinners Rowan set up, the upper echelons of the community didn't eat down here anymore, but Rowan did. He looked forward to seeing her each night, even if all he could do was sit across from her and watch her.

Much to his surprise, Cody was sitting directly across from him, next to a tall, blonde man he didn't know. Must be Sam. Cody was looking around the room, slightly alarmed as people started up with their natural voice exercise. Some even started dancing around, waving their arms in the air and shaking their heads.

When Cody's eyes found Shane's, he had to cover a laugh with a cough as he looked at him questioningly.

He could almost hear Cody ask, 'what the fuck is wrong with these people?' Shane just shook his head and smiled before bellowing out the long om he'd perfected over the last several weeks.

Cody's eyes widened in surprise before darting around the room watching everyone. Star came up to him and started rubbing his shoulders, silently flirting. Finally, Lisa picked up her plate and started serving herself, allowing everyone to follow. Cody grabbed his plate and took his place in line behind Shane. Tonight there was a large bowl of pasta, sauce, salad, roasted beets, potatoes, and carrots. He helped himself to a large portion of everything and went back to his place, sitting his plate down and waiting.

Dinner was exactly as it was every night. With less than five minutes to eat everything, he slammed the food in as fast as he could and tried to signal to Cody to do the same. Dinner plates were whisked away and silence descended. Cody gave him a questioning look, prompting Shane to hold up his hand.

Sure enough, Lisa and Cheri came bursting in the room dressed as cooks with makeshift wigs and crude costumes, declaring war on the ants. While the two fought the ants in a painful battle, Beck came in wearing armor and a gold helmet and declared peace with the animals. The play continued with some discussion about the whys and hows of war and accepting your fate and your environment. In the end all three faced the diners, froze and shouted, "Share the planet!"

Silence followed as they filed out of the room. Soon they could hear commotion in the kitchen. Shane remembered his own time on the cooking crew and knew they were frantically serving small desserts on dishes. For some reason, no one did it ahead of time, just simply waited and then worked in complete panic trying to serve up the entire table at once.

He turned and caught Cody's face. Again, he was forced to hide a laugh with a cough and gestured for the nearest water jug. Cody looked as if he just stepped foot on Mars. Shane gave him a cool it look, he needed to play this right or he'd get the boot. Shane needed him to pull this off.

Cody looked down and sipped his own water while the three cooks passed out plates of berry pie. Now the hardest, longest part of his day — dinner conversation. His eyes roamed the table looking for Rowan, surprised to discover she wasn't there. Where was she? What happened?

Cody seemed to sense his unease and shot him a look, but there was nothing he could do until after the dreaded dinner charade was over.

"We have a long lost traveler back tonight. Sam," Lisa spoke to the table at large.

"Travelers report!" People started chanting as the tall, blonde stranger across from Shane stood and slowly made his way to the center of the room.

The diners facing away from the center of the room turned their chairs to face him.

"Hello everyone. As you know, I left here a few months ago to start a personal journey. I was," he paused as if thinking over his choice of words, "advised to take some time to think about my life and what I wanted out of it. And, as it turns out, that was some pretty damn good advice."

Shane could hear the collective sigh around the table. He wanted to roll his eyes; he didn't know who this guy was, but if he had to listen to another speech about how the great Jolly changed his life for the better, he was going to throw up berry pie all over the table.

"As I walked the roadsides of this great county, I had a lot of time to think. I thought about life, happiness, and freedom. I thought about what those concepts meant to me and how I could attain each one to its fullest."

He paused and Shane felt the tension in the room ratchet up. He didn't know why, but whatever Sam was saying was making most of his companions uncomfortable.

"But, I digress. I made my way to California. Went to San Diego and hung out there with some local surfers. Then I went north and ended up in LA working as a day laborer on a movie set. From there I met a group of people who make independent films who asked me to join their merry band. I did, of course, and that led me to several places all over California and Utah. We finished the film they were working on and I parted ways with them and made my way back here.

"What I learned is that the world is full of amazing people, of all shapes and sizes. I learned that one can, in fact, do anything one sets out to do. You just have to do it. I learned that love can be the greatest motivator of all. Love for your task, love for your work, love for another person, love for your family. Love is why I'm here."

Thundering silence filled the room, the air so thick Shane could almost see it. He didn't know who this guy was, but all of a sudden, he liked him. That was not a, 'I love Jolly' speech, that was a, 'I'm living my own life, my way' speech. Sam sat and Cody gave him a nod and smile. Looked like Cody and Sam were a lot closer than he first thought.

After about five excruciating minutes of silence, Lisa rose, signaling the end of dinner.

Shane stood. Making a big show of introducing himself to Sam and Cody, the three of them worked their way past the clean-up crew and chatted about benign topics such as the crew the next day, future projects, and plans for the next Saturday night off, all while working their way down the hall to Shane's room.

"Sam, meet Shane, my partner. Shane, meet Sam," Cody said as soon as Shane closed and locked his door.

Shane eyed Sam and nodded as Sam did the same.

"You two gonna tell me what the fuck is going down? As you can tell, I've been locked up in here with these whack jobs," Shane almost growled.

"Not until you tell me what the fuck that was at dinner? Was that a play?"

Shane smiled as Sam started to explain, "It's called a theme. We have one every night. And that chanting before dinner is called natural voice. It's just a voice exercise to get you in touch with your natural register. The movements they were all doing are called molding. It's just people being people."

Shane raised his eyebrows. He didn't even know that. No one explained that part to him before — he just figured it was part of their freak show.

"On the bus here, I met Sam. He's lived here most of his life but the moment he found the love of his life, they kicked him out. Jolly told him he needed to go on a walkabout or some shit. Sam is back on the pretense of returning to the fold, but really it's to find his girlfriend, Lina, and try to convince her to leave with him."

"So you guys got buddy buddy on the ride over, huh?" Shane asked, questioning Cody's judgment. He really wanted to talk to him alone. Did Sam know about Rob? About Rowan?

"Fuck off, Sam's clean and knows a helluva lot more than you do. Here." Cody tossed his cell phone over to him.

He took it and turned it on. Honest to Pete, he'd never been more excited to see his phone before. "Will this thing work around here?"

"It will with the SatPhone hotspot I brought with me." Cody started emptying his pockets and unloading his ankle holster. By the time he was done, there was enough electronic equipment on the bed to run a government.

"And base?" Shane asked, still not sure exactly how much Sam knew.

"Rob is in that tiny as fuck town the bus dropped us off in. We did some recon on that name you gave us. It's not good. He's wanted on felony warrants that go back to the seventies. Child endangerment, exposing himself to children, and tax fraud from upstate New York. He's also a convicted sex offender—child rape. This guy is bad. How in the hell he can just be out here for all these years is fucking amazing. When we read the reports, we were like, what the fuck people—it's not like he left the states. Those papers Rowan found must not be the public records." Cody ranted and Shane needed to calm him down.

He belly laughed as loud as he could, gesturing to the rest to do the same. Soon all three were laughing like hyenas.

When they quieted down, Shane waited and shook his head.

"Last time things got weird, I found people outside my door all night. You need to keep your voice down."

"Got it. Sam, you find Lina?"

"Yup. She is so exhausted she can't think straight. They took all of her teachers and moved them to other crews, she still has about twenty kids down there, and they cut her food budget."

"Jesus."

"You said it. I'm headed over there now. Some of the others are sneaking back to help with bed time and dinner clean up. I'm hoping to grab a few minutes alone with her tonight."

"Speaking of alone time, I didn't see Rowan at dinner. Does she eat somewhere else?"

"Not usually. I need to go find her and make sure she's okay."

"Okay, well, they gave me a room of my own. Why don't I go out there and distract anyone checking up on you two. But you're on your own when you get back."

"Sounds like a plan. And Cody, It's fucking great to see you, man."

Cody smiled at him, "Yeah, Rob's a pussy on stake outs. It's time you came home."

. . .

Standing by the open window, Rowan thought of freedom. Freedom from Jolly, freedom from her mother, freedom from herself. She felt more trapped than ever and the most depressing thought was now she knew that no matter how far she ran, she could never escape her own mind. The voices in her head, the memories of the things she had done, the lives she had ruined, no amount of running would ever allow her to escape her own reality. The past was unchangeable, immutable. There was nothing she could do to change who she was and what she had done.

Shane's head popped up at the window, startling her.

"Are you okay? You weren't at dinner," he asked.

She smiled for the first time all day and stepped back to let him in.

"Not the best day for me. Had a run in with Eden."

"Eden? What about?"

"About the fact that she hasn't gotten over every mistake I've ever made." Rowan sighed and sank onto the bed.

Shane closed the curtains and followed her.

"Okay. I guess she takes that mother hen thing pretty serious, then."

Rowan scoffed, "Mother hen? Eden? Um, no. She stopped being my mother years ago."

Shane froze, "What? Eden's your mother?"

"The one and only."

Rowan watched as Shane rose from the bed, red faced. She had never seen him so angry before. His shoulders were hunched up around his ears, his muscles bulging, his hands in tight fists as he paced the room, bouncing on his toes.

"Shane."

He blew out a long breath between his teeth, "I guess it's a good thing I didn't know that before now."

"Yeah, I think so. It's okay, Shane. She hasn't been my mother in years. I've seen her discipline other people before, I just forgot what it's like. She hits hard and straight to the core."

"What the fuck did she say to you?" Shane growled at her.

"Oh, just the usual. I'm a complete waste, I've ruined everything. I'm ungrateful, useless, and generally a horrible person."

"You've ruined everything? You're a waste? She can't be serious, can she?" Shane turned back and joined her on the bed.

"Well, according to her, I was about to become a

wild, crazy, slutty teenager and Jolly was only trying to save me and our community by marrying me. And I threw away that opportunity. And became a slut anyway."

"Okay, just stop. Just fucking stop right now. That is complete bullshit. You don't believe that, do you? You need to stop talking, because if you say anything else along those lines, I'm gonna really lose my shit." Shane was up and pacing again.

His anger was too much for her. She couldn't fight Shane or even deal with his emotions. She needed to be alone and quiet. She fought the tears that formed behind her eyes, but lost the battle as they spilled over and ran down her cheeks.

"Rowan, no. You can't believe what she's telling you." Shane raced to her side.

"I don't know what to believe anymore. Everything is so messed up. I just, I can't stop hearing her scream at me. I've never screamed at Justin the way she screamed me. It's not hard to love your own kid. What is so wrong with me?" She was sobbing now and felt Shane's strong arms hold her tight against him.

"Rowan. Nothing is wrong with you. Therein lies the whole problem. You are the only sane person here. Your mother, Jolly, Storm, Jewel — they're all insane. As in not right in the head."

She knew he was right, but getting there was hard. She remembered a time when she believed it, when she was so clear on that she took her young son and ran with barely enough money to last a year and hardly a plan.

Sitting up straighter, he loosened his arms around her. His hands cupped her face while his thumbs wiped away her tears. She felt her resolve reforming. He was right, these people were ill. No real mother turns their back on their child. Something happened to Eden along the way, she didn't want the same thing to happen to her.

Nodding her head, she smiled through her tears. His face hovered close to hers, his lips grazing hers. Once, twice, three times. She reached out and grabbed him on his third pass, holding him close to her. Leaning in, demanding a real kiss.

"Rowan, I love you. That hasn't changed and never will. You are easy to love. Don't give up on us. If you give up on yourself, you give up on us. Please, don't give up."

She took a shaky breath and nodded her head, smiling.

"There was this guy at dinner. His name is Sam and he gave this speech. A traveler's report."

"Oh, and I missed it. Darn. I love Sam. He and Lina were a hot item before Jolly sent him away to punish Lina."

"Yeah, I know. He met Cody and Rob and teamed up with us to get Lina the hell out of here. In his speech he talked about love. About how love is the greatest motivator of all. Baby, I love you and I've been in this hell hole for too long. I think it's time to leave. Don't you?"

Rowan's heart felt like it was glowing. Suddenly there was no one left in the world but the two of them. "I love you, Shane. And God yes, please let's get the fuck outta here."

Shane's head snapped up and a sexy grin spread across his face, "Whoa! That's what I'm talking about." Shane wrapped his hand around her head, his thumb caressing her cheek. Breathing in his scent, she both relaxed and electrified at the same time.

"You know what I want?" he asked her, his voice thick and deep.

She shook her head.

"I want you in my bed, in my apartment. I want to wake up wrapped around you in the mornings. I want you in my kitchen making coffee, naked."

Rowan giggled, "Naked, huh?"

"Yup. I want to walk in my kitchen smelling amazing coffee and find your beautiful body taking your first sip."

He nuzzled her hair, barely brushing his lips across the soft skin under her ear. Shivers ran up and down her body as his hand clasped her head harder. She felt his other hand grab hold of her hip, bringing her closer to him.

"I want, no, I need you there, Rowan. I need to hold you all night long."

His lips finally found hers, slowly at first, but quickly he was devouring her. She heard moans from deep in her throat as his tongue demanded entrance to her mouth. Heat flew from her very core to her extremities.

She pulled her arms from around his neck to start working on the buttons of his shirt. Soon his muscled chest and strong abs were revealed to her. Say what you will about living here, the physical labor Shane had been doing for the last several weeks had morphed his already sculpted body to that of a professional weight lifter.

His stomach was a dark bronze, accentuating his bulging pecs and shoulders. His arms were strong and his biceps were huge. Wrapped in them, she felt safe and loved. Running her hands over his tight skin, she felt him shiver under her touch.

"Off, off," he moaned, pulling at her clothes.

Pulling off her shirt and flinging it somewhere in the room, his eyes lit up taking her in. Without wasting any time, she tugged off her jeans and panties and soon stood before him naked, just as requested.

He stepped back while unbuckling his belt, sucking in a breath, "You are the most beautiful woman I have ever seen. And sexy. And strong."

"Okay, okay. Enough with all that," Rowan cut him off.

"Hell no," he told her as he wrapped himself around her and moved her toward the bed, "Never enough of that. I'm just telling you the truth. The truth you should believe. You are amazing. And the best part about you is that you are mine."

"Yours, huh?" Rowan gasped out, so stunned she almost choked on her words.

"Yes Rowan. You are mine. Now and forever." Shane pushed her back on the bed and covered her with his body.

Her eyes rolled in the back of her head. This is what she needed—his weight on her. She loved feeling him on top of her. He cocooned her head with his arms and moved her hair out of her eyes. His eyes were shining dark pools of chocolate as they locked in on hers.

"Rowan, you have no idea how happy you made me the day I met you. I can't wait to get you out of here and take you home with me. Are you in?"

"I'm in, Shane."

His mouth plunged down on hers, kissing her so hard her head started to spin. His knee moved her thigh up, giving him the space he needed. Without breaking his kiss, he moved his hips back and pushed himself inside of her, electrifying her entire body.

Arching up off the bed, she met his next thrust with her hips, allowing him to go deeper, harder. Her skin felt like a light bulb, brightly burning so intensely she thought she might ignite as he relentlessly continued his onslaught. Wrapping her legs around his waist, she held on.

He sat up on his knees, hiking hers around his hips and grabbing her waist with both hands.

"Exquisite," he mumbled before starting again, slamming his hips into hers.

Rowan felt completely exposed in this position. He was looking down on her, her legs open, wrapped around him — nothing to hide. When their eyes collided, her breath stopped. As if he was looking straight through her most hidden depths, he stared into her eyes. Finally, a grin spread across his face and he picked up his pace.

The orgasm hit hard and fast, clenching down around him. Her hips flew higher, her head digging into the bed. Reaching for a pillow, she shoved it over her face to muffle a scream just before it was ripped from her throat.

"Oh, shit." Shane held her tighter, holding her while the pleasure rocked her body. "Rowan. I'm going to come, baby."

He loosened his grip and went back to his ferocious pumping before he too was overcome. She heard him attempt to hold back his loud moan, unsuccessfully. Felt him shudder as he unleashed his release inside of her before collapsing.

CHAPTER EIGHTEEN

"This is bullshit. We should take her and walk the fuck out of here. What the hell are they gonna do?" Cody asked on their way to morning crew.

"They'll fucking take her again. I don't know what happened to her those first few weeks, but I don't think it was great. When I first saw her, she had bruises all over her neck. That bastard tried to choke the life out of her," Shane answered, keeping his voice low.

"Jesus."

"Tell me about it. We need to be smart about this and move when Rob gets his shit together. We need to contact him."

"So, just to be clear, we need to make sure this Jolly guy goes away, for good?"

"Yup."

"Okay, well let me think on that. I've got some ideas, but you won't like any of them."

"Hey guys, wait up!" Sam called from behind them.

Cody and Shane turned at the same time, waiting for Sam to catch up with them.

"Hey man, have a good night?" Cody asked him.

"You could say that," Sam told them, smiling.

Shane laughed quietly, thinking about his own night with Rowan.

"So, how long before this big plan of yours takes hold?"

"We were just talking about that," Cody answered him, "Looks like we might have some time to kill, but I say we up the ante and make sure all the dirty laundry gets out."

Shane sucked in his breath; he didn't like the sound of that, "Well hold on there, Cody. We need to talk this through and figure out where Rob is before we start some shit in here."

Cody laughed, "Told you."

"Okay, I'm in, whatever it is. But just so you know, Lina knows what's up and she's scared. She wouldn't tell me everything, but whatever happened to Rowena freaked her out."

Shane's head snapped around, "What do you mean?"

"She wouldn't say, just that if we run, we need to run far and never let our guard down. Cause if he brings you back, you'll never be the same," Sam told them quietly as they walked along the path.

"Shit," Shane muttered under his breath, "This man needs to be stopped once and for all."

They had almost arrived at the crew. He could see Beck and Fern getting ready, setting out tools and going over their plans. The barn was huge and their plans were elaborate, well beyond anyone's skill level there. But around here, guts, hard work, and stupidity seemed to outweigh skills and know how.

"Later," Shane barked at them and took a deep breath, psyching himself up for another long day of crew work.

• • •

Rowan walked into the records room, gearing up

for another few hours pretending to be enthralled with budgets and ledgers. She had found what she was looking for the first time she was left alone and soon discovered that, like everything else around here, the budgets and proposals were pure fiction. Sitting in this room checking off budgets to reality was agitating at best.

Cheri was already here and she sucked in her disappointment with her breath.

"Good morning," she said, as brightly as she could.

Cheri turned slowly, absorbed in some file toward the back of the room.

"Are you ready, Rowan?" Cheri asked her.

"Um," she started, *did Cheri just call her Rowan?*

"Cause I gotta tell you, I'm really tired of waiting around for your sorry ass. If it wasn't for your sister's insistence that you're the feisty one, I'd have given up weeks ago."

Rowan's jaw dropped open. "You've been talking to Talia? Since when?"

"Since I was born, Ro. You really need to get better at reading between the lines. Now come on, I just opened this file and we have our work cut out for us."

Rowan felt like she was underwater. Was Cheri really telling her what she thought she was? All this time, she had been talking to Talia.

"You told her I was here. That's why they knew, but it took you a few weeks to get the message to her," Rowan whispered, as her world view shifted.

"Come on. We don't have all day. I just found a file detailing large quantities of weapons. Look at these sales receipts, all made by Jewel. All cash. None of the weapons we have down in the bunker are permitted or even legal. I'd bet all of them were bought from thugs."

Rowan snapped out of it and rushed to read the file.

"You didn't honestly think they went out and permitted any of those weapons, did you?"

"Yeah, I did. We all had to fill out permits so we could buy guns. It took weeks of paperwork, then Jewel spent almost a year traveling around buying guns at shows with our paperwork. So yeah, I did."

"So these are in addition to what's down there? More of them?" Rowan asked, flipping through the file some more.

"I have no idea. But whatever is going on, we have way more weapons than anyone let on. Look at the list. Hand grenades, machine guns, ammo, and this stuff, I have no idea what any of this is."

"Neither do I, but I know someone who might."

"Shane? Yeah, from what I hear, that sexy PI knows a lot about a lot of things."

Rowan flipped her head toward Cheri.

"Yeah, I know all about your boyfriend. You guys are not as quiet as you think." Cheri smirked at her, her eyes twinkling.

"Oh my God. Does anyone else know?" she whispered.

"Nope. But they might think you like to masturbate. Like, a lot." Cheri hardly contained her laughter.

Rowan couldn't help but giggle a little too. "What? You told people I was masturbating?"

"Better that than the alternative, don't you think?"

Rowan shook her head and started going over more files. They spent the next few hours reading every acquisitions file they could find. By lunch time, Rowan was scared. There were more weapons on this property than were needed to outfit a small army. She didn't know where they were all stored and she didn't know why, but over the last five years, Jewel had spent hundreds of thousands of dollars on weapons.

What they couldn't find was where the money was coming from. As a kid, she never thought about funding the ranch, and the entire time she was a teacher, she never asked where the money came from, just that she needed some of it to run her school. Now, with what she knew, she really wanted to know where all this money came from.

Cheri packed up their files and pulled out two boxes, spreading them out haphazardly on the table and floor.

"What's up?" Rowan asked her, confused.

"Well, we've been in here for almost four hours, we have to have been doing something, right?" Cheri said with a smile and continued to spread out the papers.

Rowan tucked in one of the weapons lists into her jeans and waited for Cheri to finish. They walked out together, locking up. It was well past lunch time and the offices were empty. She was tempted to start looking in storage rooms and closets for random weapons. They were somewhere on the property; she wanted to know where.

"No, you can't just come back and think you know what's going on!" Rowan heard Lina's voice on the path before they rounded the corner to see Sam and Lina in what looked like a fight.

"Lina, it's okay. Trust me. Please," Sam was saying as Cheri cleared her throat.

Lina turned, her eyes wide at the noise. "Uh, hi guys."

"Lina, don't," Sam pulled her attention back to him.

"I'll talk to you later, Sam. Okay?" Lina said, her voice higher than normal.

Sam waited, clearly frustrated, then scrubbed his face with his hands before nodding and turning away from them.

They all watched him disappear on the path before Lina turned to them, smiling weakly, "He's back and wants. Oh my God, he wants so much!"

"He wants what's best for you. You're young, in love, and have your whole life ahead of you. Don't hide from it," Cheri told her, shocking Rowan one more time.

"I just, I don't know anything but this."

"Lina, it's better. Out there, it's so much better out there. The world is actually at your fingertips out there. The possibilities are endless," Rowan spoke low, almost whispering.

"And what about you? You're here?" Lina asked her.

"Not by choice." The words flew out Rowan's mouth before she even thought about them. And they were right, she wasn't there by choice. Her choice was Oakdale, with Shane, working at the Fresh Greens. Her choice was anything other than here.

She felt her back straighten and her shoulders relax. She felt her resolve creep back into her bones.

"We should go, girls. We don't want to be too late for lunch." Cheri wisely hurried them along the path.

She needed to find Shane and give him the list. He would know what it meant and maybe where one stored all that stuff. What scared her the most were the items on the list they didn't recognize.

The three of them walked in silence until they had to split up at the path. Without stopping, Lina turned toward the Instructary. Rowan was happy for her, but knew she was scared. She just hoped more than anything that Sam was more like Shane than Colt. Cheri nudged her along after a minute, directing them both down to the Big House for lunch.

They walked in to the sounds of lunch in full swing.

Lunch was a much more casual affair than dinner, with people coming and going. Meetings took place over cold sandwiches and salad, or whatever people made up from leftovers and their personal food.

It was a first come, first serve atmosphere and often fights erupted over leftovers. When Rowan was a kid, they had their own refrigerator so they wouldn't eat the adult food. It was often just milk and peanut butter.

She quickly made a sandwich with a small salad and walked into the dining room, hoping that Shane was there. Her heart skipped a beat when she saw him sitting with Cody and Sam. Scanning the room, her heart sank when she noticed Beck and Rio right next to their table. She'd have to come up with a distraction to get him the list. She didn't want to wait; he needed to see it.

She walked right up to the table where Beck and Rio sat, "Hi, guys. And how are we doing today?"

Beck looked up at her skeptically, "Just great, Rowena. Didn't expect to see you down here. Thought you only stayed up there with all the big leaguers?"

"What?" Is that what they thought? "Oh well, um," she said, as she tripped and fell forward.

Not her original plan, but she went with it and instead of trying to right herself she launched herself, spilling her entire plate over their table and watched as the salad scattered across their food. She then jerked her hand, holding a large glass of lemonade, and aimed it right for Beck's chest. The entire glass splashed across his chest as he jumped up, tipping back his chair in the process.

"What the hell?"

"I'm so sorry!" Rowan cried as she peeled herself off the table.

Shane was at her side in a second, "Are you okay?"

Rowan nodded and continued to profess apologies to Beck. When both Rio and Beck were wiping up the spilled liquid, she slipped the paper in Shane's hand. His eyes widened and she smiled at him. Shaking his head, he tucked it into his jeans before reaching for the upturned glass.

"There's more," Rowan whispered to him.

"More?" Shane asked, tilting his head in question.

"Yes," she hoped he would understand. "I'll work on getting the rest. But just so you know." She reached for more napkins and Shane nodded, walking away.

Rowan cleaned up the mess and went back to the kitchen to make another lunch plate.

CHAPTER NINETEEN

Shane sat back down after Rowan's charade, the paper she slipped him burning a hole in his pocket. No longer starving, anxious to be done, he inhaled his food and gestured to his friends to do the same. The sooner he got out of there, the sooner he could find out what was so important that Rowan felt the need to cause so much commotion.

He stood abruptly and cleared his plate, hoping Cody and Sam were right behind him. Without looking back, he marched to his room and slipped inside, leaving the door slightly open. Right on cue, Cody and Sam followed him through the door and locked it.

"What was that about?" Sam asked him.

"Not sure yet, but she slipped me this." Shane showed him the piece of paper as he unfolded it.

Shane started reading the list of weapons. *Holy shit, this was a serious of armory.* Everything detailed on the list was paid in cash and there was no way they could have acquired it all at once through legal channels. He felt Sam approach and read over his shoulder.

"Oh yeah, that's just the list of weapons we have on hand," Sam said after he glanced at it.

"This is common knowledge? This is serious ordnance. And a lot of it."

"Well, wait," Sam started to say, but stopped after taking the list from Shane. "No, this is different stuff. We all had to fill out permits a while ago to get our own guns, but I'm not sure if this is a list of those. This looks like different stuff."

"Let me see that," Cody chimed in snatching the paper from Sam. "This is some serious shit."

"Yeah. That's our smoking gun right there. We don't need to do anything crazy. We just need to get that list to Rob and have him pass it on," Shane stated, sounding relieved.

"Then what's going to happen?" Sam asked.

"Then Jolly gets put away and he leaves Rowan alone. She can live her life, her way."

Sam swallowed, "Okay."

"What's the play?" Cody asked.

"We get the fuck outta here, that's what. Tonight. I'll let Rowan know what's going on."

"I'm in," Sam said.

Shane looked up at him, "You wanna come with us?"

"I grew up around here. I know everything there is to know about the land and how to get to town. I can get you in and out in the same night if you want. I came back for one thing and one thing only. This seems like a good way to get it."

Shane saw the determination in his piercing blue eyes and nodded his approval.

"Alright boys, we better get back to work or we'll be accused of being negative or asleep or some shit." Cody stood and headed for the door.

Shane couldn't help but smile. It was so good to have back up with him. Somehow, all the craziness was just a bit more tolerable with Cody there.

~

After looking at what he had with him, he realized that he needed none of it. There was nothing about the last several weeks he wanted to remember. Leaving his room completely intact, he slipped out and walked down the hall to Cody's.

The door was slightly open when he got there so he slipped in and looked around. Nothing was out of place, not one thing was on the small desk, and his bed was made with what looked like hospital corners. Shane smiled at his friend's habits and glanced around the room. Cody was missing.

Just when Shane was starting to wonder what he had missed, he heard Cody and Sam in the hall. They were loud and boisterous. Not what he was expecting for the evening they had planned.

They burst into room as loud as can be. Just when Shane was going to question their behavior, Cody held up a hand as the two of them continued to laugh and joke about nothing. Shane went on high alert immediately.

Finally quieting down, Sam shut the door and stood nearby. Cody fell to the floor and pulled out his backpack full of electronic equipment. Shane watched as he efficiently gathered his gadgets and slung the bag over his shoulders. He looked at Shane and nodded, his eyes conveying a seriousness that made his hair stand up. Something was going on.

Right one cue, Cody and Sam broke into loud laughter as Sam opened the door. Shane followed suit, laughing and following as if he didn't have a care in the world. The three of them howled their way out of the building and down the path, stopping halfway down.

"Something is up. We don't know what. Did you find Rowan?"

"Yeah, just briefly. She said some bullshit was starting and she needed to be visible, but she wasn't worried about it."

"Lina said Jolly was acting really strange and she was worried," Sam told him.

"So what's up with the loud, drunk routine?"

"We needed to get out and look like we didn't know or care. People brush off stupid people, ya know. And around here, the louder and stupider the more you're ignored," Sam explained.

"So what's Jolly up to? Should we stay?"

"Who the heck knows? And no, let's go now while we can. Even if Jolly is on a war path, it will just distract everyone from noticing our absence."

"Fuck it, man, let's blow this joint. These people need to be taken care of."

Shane thought about it and Cody was right. They just needed to get out and get their shit together. They had what they needed. It was time to go.

"Let's move."

• • •

"You're all negative. Look at you people. I've never seen such a worthless group before. Whiny, sniveling, 'oh Jolly, help, we don't know what to do.' You might as well be living in World 48," Jolly yelled at them.

Jolly had been yelling at them for a while now and Rowan wondered what sparked the tirade this time.

Jolly was always on edge, but he hadn't pulled scene like this in a while. This used to be a regular occurrence; she guessed she was just naïve to think he'd stopped.

"And you!" He rounded on Jewel. "You waste all your energy with your legs wide open."

Jewel's eyes went wide and then seemed to blank out, as if she just wasn't there anymore.

"Oh Jolly, Jolly, pick me, pick me. I'll do anything." He mocked her in his high, whiny voice. His face was an inch away from Jewel's, his eyes bearing down on her.

Jewel didn't flinch, barely breathed, and without warning Jolly punched her hard and fast in the gut. She doubled over with a loud umph, her eyes bugging out.

"You had so much potential, but just like all you American sluts, you get a little energy, a little knowledge of The Work, and you throw it all away," he continued screaming at her, his mouth now touching her ear.

Rowan's stomach tightened. She now knew what the problem was. Jewel obviously picked up another lover without Jolly's consent. Looking around the room she tried to catch Cheri's eye, but she wouldn't look at her. Her eyes were cemented to the floor, not looking at anyone.

It was an interesting group to have gathered. She saw Beck and Rio here as well as Star and Eden. Storm, Cheri, Jewel, and Colt were all expected, but those three were a surprise. Thank God Lina was still absent. That Instructary continued to do exactly what it was set up to do, protect its occupants, teachers, kids, and pets. Everyone who lived there escaped most of the worst that happened out here.

"There is only so much I can do for you people. I'm trying to help you here, and you won't even meet me half way!" he bellowed to the room at large. "Why are you even here?"

He walked to Beck, "Why, Beck? Why are you here?"

"Um, I'm here to work and to um, do my part, um—" Jolly's swift and harsh fist cut him off. Beck stumbled and coughed.

"Jesus. You'll never be nothing but a donkey. Carry the stuff donkey, do the work donkey, clean the shit donkey." Jolly scoffed at him and moved to his next victim. "Why are you here, Star?"

"To learn about The Work," Star answered in a strong yet shaky voice.

To Rowan's surprise, Jolly laughed and lovingly patted her hair, "Yes, yes. You're still learning. You may learn forever because you're so stupid, but you're trying."

This went on forever. Jolly went around the room and asked each of them why they were there. If he liked the answer they gave he laughed and smiled, if not, his hand would strike hard and fast at whatever body part seemed closest. Rowan watched in horror as he crept his way to her.

The answer waiting on the tip of her tongue was that he kidnapped her and locked her in a box for a month, that's why she was here and no other reason. She feared she wouldn't be able to stop herself when he asked her and knew with an answer like that, he would beat her to death. He already had choked her to oblivion for smarting off to him once.

Jolly turned to look at her, his eyes blazing and his nostrils flared. His hair was flying in all directions completing the crazed, demented look of a man who has lost his mind. Rowan's heart went to her throat and her stomach flipped so hard she thought she might double over without his fist.

"And you," he growled, "You are the worst of the worst. You not only spread your legs, you flaunt your secrets and hide behind those big eyes. As if we don't all know how calculating you are. We all know exactly what you are. You."

Rowan stopped breathing, the blood rushing behind her ears making it hard for her to hear him clearly. The back of his hand caressed the side of her face, dipping down to run along her neck. She watched in horror as his nostrils flared, clearly aroused as his fingertips brushed softly down her chest.

Jolly turned back to the room, "Everybody out. Now!" he hollered.

At first, no one moved, but then Storm turned and walked out, the rest quickly following. Taking in a large breath, she felt her shoulders relax just a smidge. She turned away from him to leave.

"Not you!" Jolly spun to face her. "You stay."

Fear clung to her. Not this, not now. If he was already in a violent mood in a group, being alone with him was asking for death. Shaking, she screamed no in her head over and over again. Finally, she had enough adrenaline to move. She bolted for the nearest door, but Jolly lunged at her, wrapping his large arm around her waist. Rowan let out a gut curdling scream. She would fight this time. No longer dull with drugs or paralyzed with fear, she was going to use all her skills to fight back.

Dropping into a ball, she slipped out of his grasp and stepped back to kick him in the face, but Jolly was too fast for her. He grabbed her foot and twisted, flipping her over. Rowan braced her fall with her hands and yanked her foot out of his hands, scampering just out of reach.

"So, this is how it's gonna be now? You fighting me? Little girl, you have no idea what you've unleashed." Jolly's menacing voice sent chills down her spine.

"I don't want to fight you. I just want to go—like everyone else. Just let me go now." Breathing hard, Rowan tried to calm herself and collect her bearings as she regained her footing.

Jolly's smirk told her she was finished. He only ever used that smile when he knew he had won. Rowan tasted the bile as her stomach revolted. Fear ran thick into her blood, making her limbs heavy and her head fuzzy.

"You, child, are done fighting me. We are done with this game of yours. I am your husband and you are mine to do with as I wish. And tonight I wish for you. I'm done being the nice, patient man everyone expects me to be. You, Rowena, are taking your place by my side."

Shaking her head side to side, she felt the sob leap from her throat before she even knew she was crying. This was what she had been running from since she was twelve years old. Jolly's hands grabbed her shoulders, but she was too hysterical to notice just how close he was.

"Enough of this nonsense." Jolly's face was suddenly right in front of her. She could smell his breath and see the wrinkles around his eyes. She felt her head spin and saw only blackness around her. She opened her mouth to say no, but a scream tore through her instead.

The sting on her cheek brought her back to reality. The punch in the gut doubled her and the taste of blood in her mouth told her she had been backhanded. Sobs wracked her body as two rough hands took hold of her and forced her to move.

Utter nonsense was spewing out of her mouth, but she couldn't stop the hysteria. She knew where she was headed, back to The Box, only this time without the calming influence of drugs. This time she would be locked in and completely aware of it.

She started flinging her body back and forth, trying to escape his hold. The pain in her head told her he had her hair and held on tight, ripping parts of it out by the roots. Barely able to breathe through the pain, she stopped struggling and let him lead her to The Box.

He marched her outside and down an unfamiliar path. Finally they entered another building and walked down several stairs. Rowan was desperately looking for escape routes, but he still had her hair in his grips and held her arms painfully behind her back. Flinging the door open, he shoved her in. Rowan glared at him, bleeding, bruised, with tears streaming down her face — she felt like a deranged person.

"You will never take me. I will never submit to your will. Ever," she growled at him, breathing hard.

He smiled at her, "We'll see, my child, we'll see," before slamming the door shut.

She heard the lock slide into place and listened. Backing as far away as she could from the door, she slid down the wall, relief washing over her. She was safe in here. He left her alone and she was safe. As the adrenaline leaked out of her, the pain seeped in. Taking quick inventory, she didn't think anything was broken, but her ankle was sore and her stomach and back ached. Her face was the worst; she could barely move her face and knew the bruises were just developing.

Taking control of her breath, she closed her eyes and prayed like hell that Jolly wouldn't go after anyone else tonight.

CHAPTER TWENTY

The slide of the lock woke her. Scooting back as far from the door as possible, adrenaline making her heart race, she readied herself for another fight. The door slowly opened.

"Rowena? Are you in here?" Colt's whisper took her by surprise.

"Colt?"

He walked in and set something down, "I'm gonna turn on the light, okay?"

"Okay," Rowan croaked out, her throat dry as sandpaper.

The light flipped on, making her eyes blink rapidly. How long had she been in here?

"Jesus Christ. What the hell did he do to you?" he said, coming back in the room.

"He beat the shit out of me, like he always does. What about you? I saw you get it pretty hard a few times back there. Was that last night? Please tell me that was only last night?"

Colt sat down and opened a bag, spilling out what looked like first aid supplies. "Yeah, it's about four in the morning. Everyone is finally asleep, but it looks like three guys took off."

"Took off? Who?" Rowan knew the answer to that question, but she didn't want to blow her cover. At least her mind was cognizant enough for that.

"Sam and two new guys. After Jolly left you in here, he went on a rampage and wanted everyone up and working. We did an all call, and found their rooms empty. Only one of them looked like they cleared out, Sam and the other guy, Shane, had all their stuff in their rooms. Jesus, let me look at you."

Colt scooted towards her and lifted her face, "You've got some pretty nasty bruises, but only a few cuts. Here, hold this on your cheek."

He handed her a cold pack. Instantly her cheek felt better.

"We could hear it, ya know. We left, but some of us waited to find out what was going on with you. I heard it. Your screaming, his yelling. You were right to leave when you did."

"A lot of good that did me."

"Yeah, about that. I didn't know what they were going to do. I was just invited to come on a trip with Jewel and then—"

"You didn't know? Colt, listen to you, you came to my house and you kidnapped me. You brought me here. You lied to me and told me Justin was here."

"I didn't say any of that. That was all Jewel."

"Really, Colt? You know what, it doesn't matter. What the hell happened? Did you and Jewel start up again?"

"No, Jewel started sleeping with Beck. And in typical Jewel fashion, rubbed it in Jolly's face. Pissed him off to no end. Jewel is a nightmare."

"You think?" Rowan almost laughed, but stopped herself before the pain hit.

"So, he took Lina when he found out that Sam had

left. Berated her the whole way up the path, calling her a slut, showed her Sam's room, told her he had abandoned her, that everyone in her life will abandon her but him. That he was the only one who would ever really care for her. She was crying and freaking out. He took her somewhere. I'm going to try and find her next. Here." He handed her a water bottle.

"Did he hit her too?"

Colt looked at her like she was an idiot, "Do you have to ask?"

"Shit."

"Yeah, drink. I'll be back when I can. It might be awhile."

"Colt," Rowan spoke when he stood up, "Thanks."

"After everything, it's the least I can do."

Rowan waited while he gathered his supplies and walked out. The lock slid into place and the light went out, plunging her into complete and total darkness.

~

Rapid footsteps outside her door woke her. Disoriented and sore, she had no idea how long she had been locked up. The lock snapped open and she bolted to the back of The Box, her heart hammering in her chest. Readying herself, she was almost relived to feel the rush of adrenaline surge through her blood, clearing her mind and tensing her muscles.

"Rowan. I'm going to turn the light on," Colt's whispered voice came through the door as it opened slightly, causing her to sag against the wall. The light flooded the room, blinding her temporarily.

"What's going on? How long have I been in here?"

Colt slipped inside and handed her a bag. Rowan reached in and took out a few sandwiches and another bottle of water, as well as a bottle of pain reliever.

"About twenty-four hours. I haven't found Lina yet, but I think Jewel has her somewhere. We've all been in retraining. Jolly's new program. We did Saturday Exercise as well as mat work. All friggin' day. Ugh."

"Jesus. No word from Lina, huh? Can you just let me out?"

Colt smiled, "Really? And how do you think that will affect the group. Jolly is already on a war path, you walking out of here will just make things go nuclear."

"Psst," she blew through her teeth, knowing he was right, but frustrated as hell.

"Eat."

She took out one of the sandwiches and took a large bite. Her jaw was still extremely sore, so it was slow going, but her body definitely needed the nutrition.

"What time is it?"

"Almost midnight. It's good out there. People are waking up. Jolly's right, we had all fallen into a slumber. I know it was bad, but the fall out is really helping the group. A couple more days of this and we can all get back to our crews, but we'll be smarter, better."

Rowan watched him and noticed the spark in his eyes and the excitement in his voice.

"Colt, how can you say this is a good thing? I'm locked up, bruised. Lina is missing. Seriously, how is any of this good?"

He turned to her and watched her, "That's the difference between us Rowena, what you see as oppression, I see as freedom. What you feel as being boxed in, I feel as safe space."

"So, me being locked up is your freedom? Boxed in? Are you kidding me? What is safe about this?"

"You know, it's not all about you, Rowena. The rest of us, we're here because it works for us. You, in this closet, yeah, that is a little over the top. I'll give you that. But I'm not talking about being locked up in here. I'm talking about living in this community. I know you hate it, you always have, but the rest of us love it. It's not just about Jolly, I'm here for the community."

Rowan was quiet as she finished off her first half sandwich. She swallowed and drank the rest of her old water bottle, knowing she had more.

"So all that time we planned on leaving? All those late nights talking about what our life would be like outside? What was that?" she asked, her voice pained.

"I wanted that so much, Rowena. I wanted to be by your side the whole way, but I just couldn't. I told you, I needed this too much."

"Is Jolly that amazing and I just don't see it?"

Colt shook his head as if thinking, "No, Jolly can be pretty scary, but it's not about Jolly, not really. Most of us are here because this system works. We better ourselves, know the rules, get to work on some great projects. Think about it, you started your own school at fifteen. You can't do that out there!"

"I was also forced to have a child at twelve, so does that still count?"

"That was your choice."

Rowan tensed and looked around her box. She would never understand him and, it would appear, he would never understand her.

"For the record, I had Justin so I didn't have to marry Jolly. Remember that detail? At the ripe old age of twelve, I didn't want to become some forty year old's wife."

"Whatever, Rowena. The point is, this doesn't work for you. I get that now. I'm sorry I helped bring you back. You need to leave, but just because you don't like it here, doesn't mean it's some evil, horrible place."

"Well, from where I'm sitting, it looks pretty damn evil and horrible."

He said nothing, just nodded his head and started to stand.

"Colt, I get that you're leaving me in here, but I'd really love it if you could keep Jolly away from here. I'd rather not get raped and beaten tonight."

"Jesus, Rowena. Is that what you think is going to happen?"

"Did you not hear him?"

He laughed a little, "You're crazy. No way Jolly would ever do something like that. Relax, everything is going to be fine. I'll come back when I can with more food. Oh, here," he reached in his pocket and pulled out a flashlight, "thought this would help a little."

With that he walked out and locked the door. Just as she figured out how to turn the flashlight on, the overhead light snapped off. Rowan shook her head and almost laughed. Even Colt, after everything he knew, everything he saw or heard, didn't believe her when it came to Jolly.

She was grateful for the food, but was worried beyond belief about Lina. Lina had never been in The Box, as far she knew, and was usually left alone. She hoped like hell she was okay. In the meantime, she opened the small bottle of pain reliever and took two capsules. That should help relieve the pain in her jaw and allow her to eat the rest of her food. She needed her strength; the next time someone opened that door, she was getting out.

CHAPTER TWENTY-ONE

Let's get this show on the road! Shane was more anxious than he'd ever been in his life. This had taken entirely too long and he was worried about Rowan. He didn't know if it was just because he hadn't seen her in a while or something else, but he had been walking around with an ominous feeling deep in his gut for the last couple of days. Now that he was this close to ending this, he wanted this shit to start.

The agent in charge was slow and methodical. Knowing just how many weapons were on site and how well trained these people were, they were double and triple checking everything. It was getting on his last nerve.

"Okay folks, let's gather up one last time." Agent Clark called her troops over. "The convoy will go in first and if all goes well, they'll let us serve our search warrant. We need the three from the compound in the front cars to direct us to the correct facilities. That's when the fine officers from Yavapai County will start collecting the civilians. We need every one of them accounted for and secured before our men approach the buildings."

The group broke up and started piling into trucks and large SUVs.

"Adams, you ride with me."

Shane didn't need to be told twice to ride shotgun on this raid. He loaded his gear into the SUV and slipped into the front seat as the rest of the crew piled in the back.

"So, you know Sergeant Brooks, huh?"

"Yes, ma'am. We've worked together a time or two."

Clark grunted and started the car. She slowly started moving forward and it took every ounce of self control for Shane to not bounce in his seat and scream 'faster faster!'

"So when your boy, Rob, called, I wasn't really that inclined to look into this mess. We've known about the compound for years, but they seemed to stick to themselves and never really caused any trouble."

"Okay," Shane answered her, not sure where this was going.

"But when Brookes called and vouched for you, I thought, well okay, let's see what the boys have. That inventory list did it, though. I really wish I knew more about what we were walking into."

"Nothing good, ma'am."

Clark was quiet the rest of the ride, leaving Shane to his thoughts. He had too many rolling around in his head, and knew he needed to pull his shit together or he was going to fuck up. He blew out a deep breath when the SUV crested over the hill and turned, opening up their view of the property.

As the convoy approached, he saw people running from building to building. Before they even parked in front of the Big House, people were spilling out, watching the line of large, black SUVs and trucks wind their way into the driveway and park near various buildings.

Clark waited, listening to her earpiece, as her men got into place. After what felt like half an hour, but was probably more like seven or eight minutes, Clark turned to him, "You ready?"

"You have no idea."

Following Clark's lead, he opened the door and stepped out of the SUV, his black wind breaker with ATF on the back simmering in the sun. He watched as Clark walked up and approached the first group of people. Beck stepped forward and took the warrant. The sheriffs surrounded the group, guns drawn and ready.

After a quick discussion, Beck gestured toward the Arena. Clark turned and raised an eyebrow at Shane. *No fucking way.* Shane only shook his head quickly. He knew there were a lot of weapons in the Arena, but he didn't know where else they were stored. They were better off holding everyone outside, away from all the buildings, but that would be pretty uncomfortable.

When Shane figured out the perfect place to hold everyone, he jogged up to Clark, nodding at Beck and watching his face take in the ATF jacket. *Whatever, fucker.*

"This guy here says we should all gather in the Arena," Clark stated.

"Arena's no good. Tell him to go to the new barn. Nothing down there but a shell of a building, but it has a roof and a clean floor. There are kids down the path and offices up that way." Shane could feel the cold stares of the group watching him, he even heard a few gasps as people recognized his role in this raid.

Clark nodded and spoke into her radio. Shane led the large group down the path and toward the new barn, keeping his distance from his old crew mates; he did not want to get into it with them right now. He simply wanted to show the locals where the holding cell was going to be and go find Rowan.

They reached the barn and everyone piled in. Shane stood back, not wanting to engage in conversation with anyone. When everyone seemed to be situated, he turned back toward the main buildings in search of Rowan.

The deputies spread out in unison, clearing each living area, taking people out in small groups and leading them to the new barn. Shane quickly made it up to Rowan's room, but by the time he got there, the locals had already cleared the building. Running back to find the group they had gathered, he didn't see her, but he didn't see Jolly, Storm, or Jewel either. In fact, he didn't see anyone from Jolly's inner circle anywhere.

He took off at a dead run to the Arena. *Please God, not the Arena.* By the time he got over there, it was total chaos. Agents were crawling all over the building as people were being led out, hands in the air. He watched the group and still didn't see Rowan. He walked up to ask if that was everyone when he saw Storm and Eden among the group. *No Jolly, no Jewel. Damn it.*

Sam and Cody approached him, "What do we know?"

"They just cleared the Instructary, no Lina. They're bringing a small group from the main offices and then all the buildings are clear. I'm heading back down to the barn to see if I can find Lina," Sam explained to him.

Shane nodded as he followed him, hoping that Lina and Rowan were together.

"They find Jolly yet?" Cody asked as they were walking.

"Not that I know of. I did see Storm and Eden coming from the Arena."

"They'll get 'em. These guys will find every one of these fuckwits on this property."

"Unless they knew and took off?" Sam said from behind them.

"How the fuck would they know?" Cody swung around to face him.

"There's no way Rowan would have said a word," Shane added, trying to calm Cody.

"It's not Rowan I'm worried about. I told Lina what we were doing. I didn't want her to think I had just run off without her."

"Shit," Cody and Shane said together.

"What a fucking loser. Flees at the last minute, doesn't even warn his people."

"Let's just go see who they have in the barn, okay?" Shane started moving quickly to their destination.

Deputies dressed in SWAT gear surrounded the building, although their guns were holstered. The barn was eerily quiet when they approached. Stepping inside, Shane darn near choked. All of them were sitting in a large circle, meditating. Some of the younger children were in laps, and others were lying down in the middle of the room. It was completely silent. Agents stood behind them, wide stance, arms crossed, not moving, listening to their earpieces.

Shane scanned the room: No Jolly, Jewel, Lina, or Rowan. He did see Star, Storm, Eden, and even Colt. *Fuck! Where were they?* He turned on his heel and headed back out with Sam and Cody right behind him.

"Have your guys cleared all the buildings?" he asked the nearest guard outside.

"Negative. The last buildings are being cleared now. There are two buildings over the ridge that the rest of SWAT is just starting."

"Sam, where are these other buildings?"

"I'll show you."

They took off at a full run, up the hill and off the path. Shane had never been to this part of the property before. Sam ducked under some low hanging trees and rounded a corner. Shane followed his movements and was shocked to see two large, industrial size buildings in the clearing. He never even knew they were there.

Agents were crawling over the buildings, guns drawn and ready. The search was well organized and obviously practiced. He watched as they used hand signals and communicated among themselves. Shane glanced over at Cody and nodded.

"Never gonna happen. I'm not going to let Rob use hand signals with us, he's bad enough with his police jargon as it is."

Shane chuckled and turned back to watch the search. Suddenly there was noise coming from inside. Without thinking, he took off. He didn't know why, but he knew Rowan was in there, and something was wrong. Thank God he had his ATF jacket, or else he would have been shot for sure.

He bolted through the door and listened for more noise.

"Ma'am, put the gun down and come with us."

Shane ran toward the voice. Three hallways and a flight of stairs later, he found the commotion. Jewel was in front of a room with her gun drawn, her hair wild with black curls, her eyes huge and her chest heaving with uneven breath. She looked completely insane and it scared the living shit out of him.

"Jewel. Listen, you need to do what these men are telling you. They are very serious and you are alone down here. Everyone else is in the new barn waiting for the search to end. Just put the gun down and come with them," Shane spoke to her behind the agent closest to her.

To his surprise, the agent didn't even flinch. He must have been warned via radio that he was on his way down.

"You? You're the new guy that freaked out after Saturday Exercise. What the fuck do you care about it? And why are you wearing — oh, shit." She momentarily let her hands slip at the realization that he was working with the ATF.

All the agents moved in as her hands relaxed, but she threw them back up, pushing them back.

"Fuck. You people don't give up, do you? I'll shoot all of you. Stay the fuck back."

"What's behind the door, Jewel? Is Jolly in there? Is that what you're doing, protecting him?"

"Jolly doesn't need protection from me. No, what's behind this door is none of your damn business."

"Ma'am, Mr. Mayfield and another woman were just taken into custody. You really need to put that gun down and move away from the door," the agent nearest to her spoke.

Just then, the door jerked as if someone pounded on it from the inside. "Let me out! Get me out of there. Help!"

Shane's head snapped up and he saw red; that was Rowan in there. *God damn it, they had her locked in that fucking room.*

"That's Rowan, sir, we need to get her out," he frantically told the agent.

"We are aware that a person resides behind the door."

Fuck! This shit needs to end now.

"Jewel, I'm coming over there. If you shoot me, these men will shoot you back, and there are a lot more of them then there are of you. I'd say the odds are in my favor." Shane stepped in front of the agent and walked right up to Jewel.

She was clearly flustered, pointing the gun at him and then back at the agent. If Shane timed it right, he could be within reach when she aimed the gun back at the agent. He kept walking, slowly, pacing his steps, watching. She pointed the gun in his face. At this range, he'd be dead the minute she pulled the trigger.

The agent stepped forward and she swung her gun toward him. Perfect. Shane stepped up to her sideways and grabbed the gun, ripping it from her hands. Within seconds the agents had her pinned to the ground and handcuffed. He ran to the door, scanning the knob for locks.

"Rowan! It's Shane, are you alright?"

He saw a switch and a deadbolt. He slid the deadbolt and yanked the door open. His breath stopped when he saw her. She was alone in the dark, in a room smaller than a closet. The Box. This is where Jolly had locked her up before. Rowan saw him and launched herself at him, wrapping her body around his.

"Shhh, baby. I got you. I got you," he told her, burying his head in her hair.

His hands came up and stroked her head and he heard her whimper. He pulled her face back to get a good look at her in the light, "Jesus fuck! Did he do this to you?"

She was covered in bruises. One side of her face was deep purple and her eyes were black and yellow.

"It doesn't matter. Let's go. Please, let's go," her voice was weak and cracked.

"How long have you been in there?" He carried her away from the room, while the agents swarmed in and cleared the rest of the area. Jewel was screaming nonsense as she was taken away, but none of that mattered. What mattered was in his arms.

He walked back the way he came. Knowing that there was at least one ambulance with the convoy, he was heading straight there. When he came out of the building, he saw Cody waiting for him.

"Can you walk, baby? We have a long haul back to the main driveway where the trucks are. You need medical attention."

"I think so. My ankle might be broken, I don't know, I haven't used it since I hurt it," she croaked again, breaking Shane's heart.

What the fuck happened? Once again, he had turned his back on her, and that bastard got to her. He held his temper in check and helped her try to stand. She tested it and nodded her head just as Cody joined them.

"Holy fuck. And I thought that other chick looked bad."

"Lina? You saw Lina?" Rowan asked.

"Cute blonde, with enough hair to sell? The reason Sam still breathes? Yeah, she was hauled outta there a while ago. Along with Jolly. He was in handcuffs, she was wrapped in a blanket, and Sam scooped her up the minute she got out here."

Rowan smiled, although it looked painful.

"Come on." Shane led them back to the ambulance. They arrived just in time to see Jolly and Jewel loaded into a large van, handcuffed, both spouting bits and pieces of the Constitution—at least, that was what it sounded like to Shane.

The medics noticed them and came over with medical boxes. While they looked over Rowan, Shane stood guard. Cody stayed with him, but pulled out his phone and started texting someone.

"Rob says to meet in town when we're done here."

"It could be hours still. I'm sure they're going to want a statement from Rowan. And she may need to be transported."

Cody had a frustrated look on his face. "Justin's with him. I don't think that message will go over very well."

"Shit. Okay, just tell him we might be awhile yet. But we have Rowan. Sound good?"

Cody nodded and went back to his phone.

CHAPTER TWENTY-TWO

Rowan looked around her room. She wondered what happened to all her stuff Jewel and Colt took from her apartment, but quickly realized that none of that mattered. Talia had been the keeper of most of her cash, as well as the few pictures she had of Justin.

The medics had wanted to take her to the local hospital for x-rays, but she refused. She wasn't ready to leave just yet. She knew when she left this time, she would never return. Jolly had been hauled away. She didn't know what charges would stick and how long he would be gone, but his hold over this community was broken.

Jewel was arrested, along with Storm, as the official owner of the property. Rowan was shocked that Storm owned this place; she always assumed that it was owned by the collective. After hours of sorting through permits and paperwork, they arrested a few other people, but no one Rowan would have predicted. It seemed as if the higher ups did an excellent job of protecting themselves.

"You almost ready?" Shane asked her from the doorway.

"Yeah, I'm just going to grab some extra

clothes. They took everything else, God knows where it is."

She quickly finished packing what little she needed and walked out. She still hadn't talked to Lina and wanted to find her.

"Looks like everyone who didn't get arrested is gathering in the Big House. Maybe we should go see what's going on?"

Rowan shrugged. She almost didn't care, but if Lina was there, now would be a good time to find her. They walked in silence. It was getting dark, the sun long gone, the air much cooler than before. Her head ached and her ankle was sore; she tried to remember the last time she took any pain reliever.

Walking into the Big House, she heard Eden's strong voice coming from the living room.

"I know some of you didn't agree with what they were doing, and you were probably right. But, he had his reasons. The good news is that they protected us and left us to carry on. I have faith that Jolly and Storm and the others will be back soon. In the meantime, we need to keep going, keep working, keep building. We need to stay awake."

Rowan listened to her impassioned speech, unaffected by her words and wondering how many others were. Beck stood and rallied with her, firing up the group somewhat. She was still confused about who they took and who they left. *I guess it was all about the paper trail they found.* From behind the door, she scanned the room and found Lina and Sam sitting in the corner with Cheri. Lina didn't look nearly as bad as she did, thank God.

Stepping into the room, she heard a collective gasp as people took in her appearance.

"Oh my God, look what the men with guns did to

her!" Star said, standing up and pointing to Rowan.

She shook her head, sadly. This was going to be hard. She was about to tell them that their hero, their savior, did this to her. Murmurs and chatter filled the room as she swallowed.

"It wasn't the guys with guns that did that to her. The guys with guns rescued her from a dark closet, where she had been without food or water or access to a bathroom for days. Jolly did this to her." Shane stepped up and spoke to the room at large.

"Now hold on there," Colt said, "I was taking care of her. She had water and food as well as medical care."

Shane's jaw locked down, hard, and his body tensed. "So you knew she was locked in there and kept her there?"

"No, I uh. I um —" Colt stumbled over his words.

"It's okay, Colt kept me alive. Jolly beat me and locked me in The Box at the shelters. It wasn't the first time."

"Liar!"

Rowan didn't know who yelled that, but knew they wouldn't believe her, so she wasn't surprised.

"You've always hated it here, Rowena. I don't know why you came back at all," Beck spoke up, his voice harsh.

She laughed sadly, wondering how much to disclose to this crowd.

"It doesn't matter," Eden stepped in front of her, "I think Rowena was better off outside. She'll be leaving tonight. Anyone else who wants to leave should go with her. I'll even organize transportation."

It was as if the air was sucked out of the room. No one even dared to breathe. No one had ever uttered those words before, leaving was never an option, for anyone — it was a threat or a punishment.

Slowly, Cheri stood, "I'd like to leave."

Before the room even had time to react, Lina and Sam stood together, "We're leaving," Sam spoke.

Eden waited; no one else moved. Rowan was disappointed, but in her heart, she knew she should've expected it. These people had lived their whole lives here, some of them born and raised, what else did they know?

After a minute or so, Eden cleared her throat, "If that's all, the five of you need to leave now. Get your stuff together, you have until midnight."

Without hesitating, Lina, Sam, and Cheri walked toward her. Rowan couldn't help the smile spreading across her face — she was free. After this, no one would come after her, or any of them.

~

"Can you believe that prick? Standing up in front of everyone and saying you were fine in there. That you had food and water and medical attention? What an ass." Shane's jaw worked overtime as they sat in the back of the old Nissan that brought him to the property in the first place.

"Well, truth is, without Colt, no one would have come. Usually Jolly is the only one who brings me food or water in there. At least there was a bucket for, ya know. But man, it was bad."

"Jolly was with me," Lina told them from the front. "He kept me in his room and locked me in his bathroom when he left. He wanted to know where you were, Sam. What you were up to? People came in and out all the time, but he never let up. And then we ran to the shelter with Jewel."

"Did he um, are you okay?" Sam whispered to her.

"He hit me like usual, but nothing more."

Sam blew out a breath he was holding and stroked her hair as he drove along the dark road.

"I'm sorry, guys. I tried to find you, but Colt wouldn't tell me where you were and things were nuts," Cheri said.

"Seriously, it's fine. We survived, we're out. I can't wait to call Justin."

"We're meeting Cody in town, at a hotel. I sent him a text, hopefully it'll make it to him before we do."

Rowan was exhausted, but still giddy. She was off site, with Shane, and had Lina with her. Sam and Cheri seemed just as excited. The rest of them could stay on site for the rest of their lives for all she cared at the moment. You can lead a horse to water but you can't make it drink. She had shown them all what Jolly was really capable of, Shane had brought ATF agents and everyone saw the number of weapons they hauled away—the man was in jail. If that didn't crack his hold on them, she didn't know what would.

What she did know was that she was free. No more running, no more hiding, no more looking over her shoulder. She and Justin could do whatever they wanted. She got goose bumps every time she thought about it. She couldn't wait to call Justin and tell him. Talia would be over the moon, too.

Sam pulled into the hotel parking lot and they piled out. Shane led them to a room upstairs. The thought of a bed sounded heavenly.

"Where is she?" Justin's voice boomed over her as a door at the top of the stairs flew open. "Mom!"

Before she made it to the top, Justin rushed her and threw his arms around her, hugging her so tight she could barely breathe.

"Hey, hey, I'm right here," she told him, squeezing

back. "Where'd you come from?" she asked him when she pulled back.

"Come from? I've been here. How do you think Shane found you?" he said with a proud smile.

Rowan rounded on Shane, "You knew he was here and you never said anything?"

"I just didn't want—I wanted you to keep a clear head. That's all," he told her, his arms raised.

Justin wrapped his big hand in hers and pulled her upstairs where Rob and Cody were waiting.

"Hi, Rowan, good to see you. I'm so sorry we didn't cover our tracks better. I can't believe that bitch came back and followed us to Shane's. We led her straight back to you," Rob told her as he squeezed her in a hug.

"Not your fault, Rob. For all her faults, she's pretty smart. I wasn't surprised she found me. Don't sweat it."

"Oh, my God. What the hell did he do to you?" Justin pushed Rob aside to look at her face.

"Nothing that won't heal," she told him gently.

"Not to be a party pooper, but are there beds for us?" Sam asked.

"Yeah, man. Come with me." Cody led them out, leaving a much smaller crowd in the room.

"Justin, let's walk," Rowan said, "Shane, what room should I meet you in?"

"215, right next door, babe."

She nodded and walked out with Justin. When they got to the edge of the parking lot, she turned to him.

"I'm so sorry," she told him.

"You're sorry? I should be sorry. I left, and didn't send that postcard right away. I kept meaning to, but I just dove right back into life. I had all these friends there and every day was like a party. If I had sent that, you would've known they were lying."

"No, I would have still gone, just to be sure they hadn't picked you up after you had sent it."

"Well, now I have one of these," he held up his phone, "and you're getting one too, with GPS on it, so I'll always know."

She smiled at his protectiveness, "You won't have to. He's gone. In jail. And there's no way they would let me back anyway. I caused a shit storm back there." She grinned.

His eyes lit up and she could see the tension ease out of him.

"Justin, I had a lot of time to think in there. There's something I want to tell you."

He blew out a long breath, "Okay."

"I love you, Justin. From the moment I knew you were inside of me, I have loved you."

Rowan watched as tears pooled in his eyes. He looked away and scrubbed his face with his hands before turning back to her. He opened his mouth to speak, but choked on his own breath.

"Baby, it's okay. I just want you to know that no matter what happens, I love you."

Reaching out, she scooped his big body into her arms and held him close to her. She felt his body jerk as silent sobs took over. She rubbed his back and held him closer.

"I love you, mom," Justin sobbed, still buried in her neck.

They held each other for a long time before finally breaking apart. Rowan's face was wet with tears and Justin's eyes were red and swollen.

"Ah, Jesus, the guys are going to give me so much shit for this," he said, laughing while he wiped his eyes.

"Language, boy," she teased him as they walked back to their rooms.

"Hey, Mom, Did you see Hannah?"

"No, I heard her family left about a year ago. Just disappeared into the night. People said Jolly sent them to retraining, but you know, they probably just fled." She watched as Justin's jaw set before nodding. "I'm sorry. Maybe you can find her. I hear you're pretty good at that sort of thing."

They walked up the stairs and Justin turned to walk her to her room when Rowan saw Lina standing on the balcony a few rooms away.

"You go ahead inside, Justin. I'm going to go talk to Lina. Okay?"

"Okay, thanks, Mom. For everything."

Rowan turned and made her way to Lina, "Hey."

"Hi," Lina smiled sadly at her.

Rowan leaned on the railing, "You okay?"

"Yeah." She blew out a long breath, "I'm just missing my kids. I can't believe I just walked away like that. I didn't even get to say goodbye. What's going to happen to them now?"

"Honestly?" Rowan asked her.

Lina bit her lip and nodded her head.

"Nothing. They'll put Marley and Shasta back down there and life will go on."

"Yeah, but, who's going to protect them now?"

"You really think after all that the authorities aren't down there right now building files on all those kids?" Rowan paused, "You know how every summer the parents would take their kids back and we would worry 'cause they didn't know all the little things we had learned over the winter. But we had no choice, they were the parents. You can't protect kids from their own parents, Lina. You can only protect your own."

"I know," she said through tears, "It's just hard."

Rowan wrapped her arms around her friend. She

was hurting. Rowan was lucky, when she left with Justin, she left all the kids in Lina's care. Now poor Lina had no such reassurance.

"Listen, I know you're scared, but this is the best thing that could have happened to you. I promise you," Rowan told her.

She nodded again before heading back to her room. Rowan watched as she opened her room and heard Sam ask if she was okay. She knew Lina would be more than okay. It would take some time, but everything would be okay.

Heading back to her own room, her stomach fluttered with excitement. She was finally going to be able to sleep in the same bed as Shane all night. For months, she had been dreaming about being allowed to rest her head on his strong chest and wake up to his heartbeat.

Opening the door, she saw Shane sitting up in bed, waiting for her. A sexy grin spread across his face as she stepped in the room. Oh yeah, as long as she could see that grin every day, everything was going to be more than okay. She was going to be just fine.

THE END

The Escape Series Continues

ESCAPING
WITH EVE

Justin's Story (Book Four)

A full length, stand alone, romantic suspense thriller
Mysterious and riveting.

Justin Ross is old enough to know better. Five years have passed since his team took down the violent cult that raised him, but Justin still feels haunted by his unusual childhood and hurried adolescence.

Now, a college graduate and an established Private Investigator, he's tired of his past defining his future. Ready to start his own life, on his terms, a young woman shows up on his doorstep desperate for help.

Shylo is no ordinary woman and her twin sister, Eve, is no runaway. Willing to risk everything to take her case, Justin defies his own rules and follows his heart, spiraling out of control for the first time in his life.

Justin willfully ignores the advice of his team and risks everything on the case of this mysterious missing woman. When the evidence points him in a direction he knows he has no business investigating alone, he finds himself in danger, with nowhere to go but through the darkness he once fought so hard to escape.

Entrusted with an unstable new mother, her baby, and the radicalized twin-sister of the woman he loves, Justin must come face to face with the devil himself to save them all.

Read on for a sneak peek!

A Note from the Author

Thank you for reading Escape. This installment has been an incredible experience to write. If you enjoyed the series, please think about leaving a review. To be notified of new releases, get updates on stories, free books, giveaways, and more join my mailing list at www.SydneyHolmes.com/contact-sydney

My first big thank you is to you — the readers! I'm thrilled you read my book. I loved writing it and hope you enjoyed it as much as I did.

Once again, Valerie from Loud Lit Chicks, swooped in and saved the day! Thanks Valerie, your work remains invaluable.

Karen not only designed the cover, but she has been my greatest champion from the very beginning. Thanks Karen, what would I do without you?

Of course, I wouldn't be here today without my husband. Somehow I married the most amazing man on the planet. Words cannot express my love for you and all you do. Thank you from the recesses of my heart.

And last but most definitely not least, I would like to thank my amazing beta readers! Once again, you guys really rocked it! Without you, life just wouldn't be the same.

MEET SYDNEY

Sydney Holmes writes hot mysteries and spicy romantic suspense, or as she likes to say, "Hot and spicy romance that keeps you up at night!

Sydney is married to a wonderful man and they have two children. Sydney graduated from The George Washington University with a BS in Political Science and holds a Master's Degree in Education. She lives near the ocean in California and travels as often as she can.

To learn more about Sydney, please visit her website at www.SydneyHolmes.com. Or, check her out on Facebook: www.FaceBook.com/SydneyHolmesAuthor And, follow her on Twitter: @SydHolmesAuthor

For periodic updates, news, events, book releases, and sneak peeks please join Sydney's mailing list at www.SydneyHolmes.com/contact-sydney.

Excerpt from

ESCAPING
WITH EVE

SYDNEY HOLMES

CHAPTER ONE

It was almost too easy now. Picking up young, vulnerable nubiles was getting boring. Not that he'd ever tell Jace that, but every single one of them had the same haunted look in their eyes, same broken smile, same chip carried on their thin shoulders. Eve was no exception—easy to spot, easy to get close to, easy to convince. Jace would love her. She was exactly what he wanted. "Go out there and collect those that the Goddess has lost."

Not that he completely understood everything Jace did, but he knew that the man was magic, tuned in, spiritual. Jace alone was in line with what the Goddess wanted for them. And he also knew that their entire way of life—the only way to live a real life—all of their future plans, the very purpose for even being alive, all hung precariously in the wind...completely dependent on how well Reed did his job.

Well, not entirely on Reed. He knew that there were others that did what he did. But still, Reed was a soldier, forging out in the wild on his own, living amongst the dead, a seeker for the Goddess. He knew Jace had his reasons and he didn't need to know what they were—his job was to bring in these women, so that's what he did.

It's not like he was stealing them from their lives—he was bringing them home. Without him, they would remain lost and languish out here among the non-living. Jace alone understood the power these women had; he knew how to get them in touch with the Goddess, and how to change the world with their power. If not for Jace, these poor women would be lost forever. In truth, they would all be lost without Jace's guidance.

He'd seen it firsthand—how Jace could take a seemingly lost woman, what looked to Reed like a total basket case, and turn her into an enlightened being with a direct line to the Goddess. Hell, Reed himself had been lost and at war with the entire world when Jace had found him. But it was Hera that was living proof of Jace's teachings and connections. Hera was once just as lost and vulnerable looking as Eve. In fact, she was so much like Hera that Reed knew he would be rewarded for bringing her in.

"So, where are we going again?" Eve's haunted greenish-brown eyes turned to him. Her dirty blonde hair fell in messy waves just to the top of her perky breasts. High cheekbones and slightly hallowed cheeks gave her the appearance of a model—frail, with big ruby lips that made her look like she was pouting most of the time. But it all clashed with the tough girl act she tried to pull off.

"To my family. I want you to meet my family, they will love you." Reed glanced her way while driving lazily with one hand.

~

Eve couldn't believe her luck. Just when she was at

the end of her rope, end of the line, when everyone had turned against her, even Shylo, Reed walked into her life and had changed everything. Who needed her sister's approval? Not Eve. Twin or not, Eve just didn't need it.

So she wasn't the perfect one with a clear path to success; didn't mean she was a waste of time. Ha! College was for the birds, for other suckers who wanted to be stuffed inside a box and willingly submitted to thought control all day.

And Shylo wasn't perfect. My God, Shylo was so far from perfect it made Eve's blood boil! But, would anyone believe that perfect Miss Shylo had flaws like everybody else? Nope. Their fates were set in stone years ago. No matter what happened now, Shylo would always be the perfect one and Eve would always be a disaster.

But Eve knew — Shylo was just as messed up as Eve, but man, could she lie like the best of them. Their last fight had really been too much for Eve.

"Get your shit together, Eve!" Shylo had screamed at her. "You need to stop falling in love and start taking your life seriously."

As if!

Eve was no longer listening to her twin. Shylo was just as guilty of falling into bed with unrepentant men as she was. What a hypocrite! Shylo slept with her professor for a good grade, but when Eve goes out on one date with her TA, she's the one who needs to get her shit together? Screw that!

Reed had found her at her worst. When the thought of living another day in this mundane existence was so overwhelming, she was ready to jump off a bridge just to feel the water hit her skin and remind her that she was alive. After she met Reed, finishing the semester didn't seem important. In fact, living in the rat-race seemed absurd.

And, that rat-race was keeping them apart. Reed seemed to never want to be apart from her. He would wait for her outside her classes, his brown eyes looking so relieved every time she found him outside her door. Eventually, she started to feel so bad for him that she just stopped going to class.

She knew he was gorgeous by the looks the other girls gave him on their way out of class, but Reed never even glanced their way. Not once. Sometimes, Eve would wait and watch him. She wasn't stupid, she'd been duped before. Reed was the real deal.

The phone sitting on the center console rang. They both glanced at the screen only to see her own face stare back at them with the name Shylo across the top.

"I should get this." Eve moved to pick up the phone.

"Don't let her derail your joy, Eve. Remember, we talked about this. Don't let her steal your energy." He looked over at her, his face full of concern and empathy.

She simply nodded and picked up the phone, "Shy, what's up?"

"Eve! I'm so glad I caught you. I'm sorry we fought."

Shylo waited for her to respond, but Eve didn't take the bait. She was getting better at being her own person already!

"Right, so I just heard you skipped out on your last final. I talked to Mr. Ingles and told him you were sick. He said I could make it up tomorrow — well, you can."

"You pretended to be me?"

"Yeah! Well, I didn't mean to, but he just assumed I was you, so I went with it."

"Ha! That's awesome. Maybe you could take the final for me." Eve couldn't believe her twin sister did that for her. That was never her 'thing'.

"I'm not taking your final for you. Where are you? I can come pick you up and we can study," Shylo said, with what sounded to Eve like fake enthusiasm.

"Uh, no. I'm going on a road trip with Reed to meet his family."

"Eve, no! Reed? That guy you just met? This is exactly what I was talking about. You are one final away from your degree. Just tell Reed to wait one more day. If you had taken it yesterday, you would be done already."

"Stop. I'm not listening to you. I'm my own person. I'm not letting you derail my joy. Reed is perfect and I'm going to meet Jace."

"Derail your joy? What are you talking about? Dad is going to kill you. Please, Eve, just tell me where you are. I'll talk to Reed; if he has to leave, you can join him later—like in twenty four hours!"

"Shylo! I'm doing this. You can take my finals or not. You can't steal my energy. I'm with Reed now—after all the hell I went through over the years, I can't believe you're not supporting me." Eve almost stomped her foot with impatience. Why couldn't her sister just be happy for her? Why did she have to be such a killjoy all the time?

"This is the biggest mistake you have ever made. I can't believe Reed would do this to you. Twenty-four hours—just tell him you can leave tomorrow. Please don't do this, Eve. Please," Shylo begged her sister through the phone.

Eve was starting to listen to her, Shylo had always been over-protective, but there was something in her voice that made her want to listen to her. Until she felt

Reed's hand on her hip and his breath on her neck. When Reed touched her, everything else faded away.

"Say good night," he whispered seductively in her ear.

"Shylo, tell Dad not to worry. I'll see you in a few weeks."

"Eve! Eve, wait!" Eve could still hear her sister while Reed sucked on her ear and rubbed his warm hand on her inner thigh.

Reed's kisses made everything perfect in her world. Suddenly her phone wasn't in her hand anymore. They weren't in the car anymore, they weren't even on the road. When Reed touched her, she was transported to another world entirely, a place where they were the only two people alive.

"You better watch the road, mister," she finally said after she tuned back in.

"I'm going to pull over," he growled in her ear once again before sitting up.

Smiling, Eve started getting excited about where they were going — to meet his family. So soon! Okay, so it wasn't a blood family, but the way Reed described them, it was better. These people all chose to become a family, they weren't just thrown together by a freak act of destiny. Just a biologic anomaly — a malfunctioning ovary dropping two eggs. These people were committed to each other.

"I told Jace all about you and he really wants to meet you," Reed said, interrupting her thoughts.

"Jace? Right — he's like your father, but not your real father." Eve looked around, her sister's words bouncing around in her head. "I have to take that final tomorrow."

"My beautiful Eve. You don't need to take a final. I need to take you back to my house and make love to

you. I need to be inside you. That's real need, babe."
Reed leaned over and kissed her neck — sending
shivers down her spine once again.

But not enough to truly shake off Shylo's phone call.
She knew she hadn't been to her classes in a while, but
knowing that she could have taken her finals still made
her question the timing of her departure. Was she
really making the right decision?

The obligation of being a twin had always weighed
on Eve, and for years now, she had wanted nothing
more than to be her own person. Reed supported her
whole-heartedly. How could she be her own person
with Shylo right there at every turn? Reed was
adamant that Eve needed to get away from Shylo and
live on her own.

Not that it was always bad, they had some good
times for sure, but these last few weeks had been
awful. Still, late at night, she regretted fighting with
her sister. Reed was always there in the morning to
remind her of how important it was to live
independently, but she secretly missed her sister.

Reed really wanted her to find her true self — he was
such a great boyfriend. That was what she was doing,
right? Finding herself! Whenever she would get scared,
she would just remember Reed's words, "You can't
find your true path with those that want to break you
down, keep you in a box. Shylo wants you to be a
certain way — her way. You need to find your own
way."

And he was so right. She was free! It felt so good.

Reed pulled into the gas station and Eve jumped out
to find the bathroom. They'd been driving for hours
and Reed needed to go as well, but first he had an all
too important task to complete while she was out of

sight. Waiting until she walked around the corner before grabbing her phone, he first wiped out her contact list and then pulled the battery out. Moving quickly, he opened a bottle of water and soaked it, cradling the device in his hand, submerging it as best he could. Finally, dumping the water from his hands he dried off the battery as best he could before snapping it back into the phone just before Eve came back from the bathroom.

"Where are we?" she asked looking around, bewildered.

"On our way to paradise!" he said before kissing her quickly on the cheek and checking the gas pump.

"Damn it," she muttered under her breath.

"What's wrong, babe?"

"My phone died. I need to charge it. Do you have a car charger with you?" she asked pressing the buttons on her dead phone.

"No, but we can charge it when we get there. Did you turn off WiFi? I'm sure it died looking for WiFi connections en route. That last phone call was just too much for it, huh." He tsked at her with a smile.

"Yeah, I guess. Oh well." Eve looked around at the trees and the dark sky one more time before climbing back into Reed's truck.

Just as they pulled back out on the road, the skies opened up and soaked the roads with a torrential downpour. As the miles wore on, the rain became mesmerizing. As much as Eve wanted to stay awake and watch the scenery, her eyes wouldn't stay open. Soon she was fast asleep in the seat next to Reed.

Reed watched her fall asleep and couldn't be more pleased. They had at least another hour before they got to The Hacienda. With the skies this dark, the rains would saturate the roads, making them nearly impassible soon. There was no way anyone would be driving on them for at least a week. Eve was pretty smitten, so it would take at least that long before he'd be able to leave again. He didn't want to abandon her as soon as they arrived. He wasn't evil. This one needed to be passed off with care.

CHAPTER TWO

Walking down the hall, Justin couldn't believe this was the last time he was going to make this journey. This was the last assignment he needed to turn in — ever! It had been five long years, but he had done it. It was an awkward feeling finishing his degree, knowing that he wouldn't be sitting in classes and writing papers in a few months' time.

Dr. Emery, his criminal justice supervisor, had threatened to fail him if he didn't get his paper into her hands by 3:30. It was now 3:20. He'd learned years ago that his easy smile, charm, and good looks would not work on this professor. Having come out with a B in one of her classes after getting a zero on an assignment freshman year, he had never pushed his deadlines with her again.

Now Dr. Singer, his psychology supervisor, she was a pushover, and he'd been late on almost every single paper ever assigned in her classes.

"Five whole minutes, Justin! Geez, I'm surprised you didn't stop for coffee." Dr. Emery stood outside her office door.

"No, Ma'am. You know me, I might be close, but I always make it just in time!" Justin smiled at her, hoping to avoid a lecture on the benefits of being early.

"Just-in-time-Justin." She shook her head and held out her hand.

He stopped and hesitated. This was it. As soon as he turned this paper in, his tenure at UC Berkeley would be over—he would no longer be a college student. He would need to face his future and figure out what would be next for him. Decide which way to go: criminal justice or psychology. He knew a big government agency would never take him with his past, and his chances at a police department weren't much better.

"You okay?" she asked him, concern crossing over her face.

"Yeah, just wow. This," he held up the paper, "is my last assignment. This is it. I hand this to you and I'm no longer a student."

"Ah, the monumental moment when the student becomes an adult. I remember it well." She sighed and took the paper from his grip. "Do you have plans?"

"I know I'm seeing my mom at graduation."

Dr. Emory laughed, "No, I meant do you have any life plans? That fancy law firm you work for going to hire you full time?"

Justin smiled. Although he loved working as an investigator for one of the top law firms in Oakland, he was wrestling with the bigger questions that plagued him. "So far no offers have come in."

"You're a damn good investigator and you'd make a hell of a lawyer. You just have to figure out what works for you."

"Now you sound like Dr. Singer." Justin laughed.

"Well, I must admit we've talked about you. You're young, smart, a little mysterious maybe, but you have a lot going for you. Don't let your demons lead you astray."

Justin looked around the room. What did she know about his demons? He had never shared his past with anyone, making up some dream childhood and passing off his investigative skills to growing up with a stepdad who was a private eye. He did his senior thesis on mind control and used his own past as part of his research, but never admitted to having grown up in a cult.

That was nobody's business. That was something he wished he could forget about every day. He didn't want his past to define his future. He didn't want to be angry that his past stole his childhood and never gave him a chance to be an adolescent. He didn't want his demons to be the reason he was questioning his future at this very moment.

"You know me, I don't have demons!" Justin laughed it off and pulled out his charm.

"Right, kid. You're one of the lucky ones," Dr. Emory said, the sarcasm clear, but Justin wasn't about to acknowledge it.

"Well, I gotta run. Thanks for everything. I'll see you in a few weeks when I get to walk with the funny cap."

"You bet, Justin. Take care now." She smiled one last time before turning back toward her office and shutting the door.

Justin spun on his heel and walked back out of the building. He could hardly believe he was done! It happened so fast. He thought he'd have finals right up until graduation, but all of his final projects this semester were papers—massive, hard research papers that had kept him in the library every night for the past month. But, he did it. It was the beginning of May and he was done!

With no school for the next few weeks, he was looking forward to clearing his caseload and impressing his mentor. Mr. Thornton was a hardass, and Justin had been working harder and harder looking for that nod of approval the man hardly ever gave out. After seeing it a few times, Justin craved it more than he'd ever admit to anyone, even himself.

He jumped in his truck and went back to his apartment. He was one of the few students at Berkeley that lived alone, but for him it was imperative. There was no way he would ever live with a group of people again. Ever.

Honestly, he questioned how Rowan was able to live with Shane. He knew his mom was truly head over heels in love when she willingly moved in with him. It seemed that she had finally let go of the terror of their past, but Justin still checked his closets and under the bed when he got home at night, and kept a go-bag just in case.

Given his unique skill set, he was able to charge a pretty penny for his work while a college student, and many law firms were only too happy to pay. Even with his bold and somewhat cocky attitude regarding his abilities, he did feel lucky that Mr. Thornton's firm had hired him. It was that steady stream of income that afforded him the luxury of living alone, just off campus.

Berkeley was awesome. He loved living in the chaos, and the weather was so much better than in the central valley where Shane, Rob, and Cody lived. He had had every intention of moving back there to be closer to his mom, and work with Shane, but after almost five years of this weather, he just wasn't sure anymore. Hell, he wasn't even sure he wanted to work as a PI anymore.

His phone rang at his hip, interrupting his thoughts, "Yo."

"Justin, my man! You called?" Cody answered back through the phone.

"Right you are. I'm looking for someone and I thought I'd tap into your resources."

"Shoot it over, man! I'll run it through my system." Cody paused for a second. "You done yet?"

Justin laughed, "Sure am. Just turned in my last paper." That felt good to say. It was sinking in; he was done with school.

"Well done! When do we get you back?"

Justin froze. The question he'd been waiting to hear for years, and yet dreading more and more for the past few months.

"So about that. I don't... I've got a pretty big caseload at the moment. I'll see you guys at graduation. You all still coming up?"

"Uh, yeah, man. Of course."

"I thought I'd still be in school, but looks like I have a few weeks to really get ahead and be done with all of this by graduation." Justin pulled into his apartment's parking lot.

"Yeah, alright man. Send me the data and I'll see if I can at least narrow the search field for you."

"Thanks, Cody. I'm just pulling up now. I'll email you in a sec." Justin signed off and cut the engine.

The feeling in the pit of his stomach didn't set well with him. He had always asked Cody and Rob for help with his cases, but now it felt...odd. As if he was too old to be dependent on them.

Regardless, he knew Cody's database was exactly what he needed to track down the required information. And, he knew that Mr. Thornton wanted his cases closed quickly, so he had no choice. Shaking off his mixed emotions, he climbed out of his truck. Time to get to work.

Grabbing his stuff, he locked up and hurried over to the stairs, taking them two at a time — only to stop short. A woman was sitting at his doorstep. She looked up at him just as her hand brushed her shoulder length blonde hair behind her ear and wide, pale green eyes pinned him with a hopeful stare.

"Justin?" she asked. "I'm so glad I found you."